'Let's get on with our meeting . . .'

'*Our* meeting? What do you mean, *our* meeting?'

'Just that, my dear Miss Hardcastle, I'm the man you've come to see.'

'*You*?'

Just for a moment, Liza thought Richard Hawkes must be joking. But then she realised that, alas, he was deadly serious.

'You mean *you're* the owner of the castle?'

'Lock, stock and barrel!' Richard's smile had grown wider. 'Every stick and stone of it belongs to *me*!'

Stephanie Howard was born and brought up in Dundee in Scotland, and educated at the London School of Economics. For ten years she worked as a journalist in London on a variety of women's magazines, among them *Woman's Own*, and was latterly editor of the now-defunct *Honey*. She has spent many years living and working abroad—in Italy, Malaysia, the Philippines and in the Middle East.

Recent titles by the same author:

LORD OF THE MANOR
DANGEROUS PRETENCE

COME BACK FOREVER

BY

STEPHANIE HOWARD

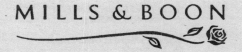

MILLS & BOON

MILLS & BOON and the Rose Device
are trademarks of the publisher.
Harlequin Mills & Boon Limited,
Eton House, 18-24 Paradise Road, Richmond, Surrey, TW9 1SR
This edition published by arrangement with Harlequin Enterprises B.V.

© Stephanie Howard 1994

ISBN 0 263 78781 8

Set in Times Roman 11 on 12 pt
01-9506-48576 C

Made and printed in Great Britain

CHAPTER ONE

THERE was a loud, ominous tearing sound at the back of Liza's jeans as she adjusted her position in the fork of the tree in an effort to obtain a better view of the castle.

'That's what you get for trespassing!' she chastised herself with a wry smile. And though she was curious to know just how bad the damage was, she didn't dare release her grip on the tree-trunk. As it was, she was feeling quite precarious enough, perched up there among the branches. Climbing trees definitely wasn't Liza's forte! She'd never had much of a head for heights.

But at least her efforts hadn't been wasted. She'd got what she'd been after—a splendid view of the castle. As she gazed at it from her vantage point at the edge of the wood, with a clear view out over the lawns and gardens that encircled it, Liza felt a fierce surge of emotion whip through her.

So this was Abbotsdale Castle, which she'd heard so much about, the background to all her Great-aunt Julia's magical stories. And it was even more amazing than she'd expected.

She paused for a moment to admire it, her green eyes drinking in its turreted splendour, the centuries-old walls covered in ivy, the ancient stone parapets and the lead-framed windows that twinkled in the gentle Yorkshire summer sunshine.

5

'Aunt Julia, how I wish you could be here to see it! It's everything you ever said it would be, and more!' she breathed.

Then she smiled to herself. This beautiful place had once been the home of the wicked Hawkes family, the scourge of her own and Aunt Julia's family, the Blakes. But that had been long ago. The Hawkeses had long gone and the castle these days had fallen into less villainous hands.

At least she hoped that was the case, Liza thought to herself, smiling. She was hoping to persuade the new owners to let her have a look round!

It was at that moment that there was a rustling in the woodland behind her. Startled, Liza spun round, catching her jeans in the branch again, and once more there was the sound of tearing denim. But this time Liza took no notice. Suddenly, all her attention was fixed elsewhere.

For coming towards her was a dark-haired man on horseback. And though she couldn't see his face—she was looking down on him—there was something about him, some powerful commanding quality, that kept her eyes fixed to him like magnets.

Perhaps it was the way he sat so straight in the saddle, his feet in their shiny boots resting easily in the stirrups, his strong thighs lightly gripping the sides of the black steed, or perhaps it was the set of the broad, muscular shoulders, carelessly self-assured beneath the dark green sweater, but he had an aura about him that sent strange shivers through her. She found herself longing to look into his face.

Fool, she chastised herself. That's the last thing you ought to want! The best thing that could happen is that he doesn't even notice you, so that you can get out of here without being caught!

And for the moment, she was pretty certain, he hadn't seen her. Perched halfway up the tree, she was out of his line of vision. And it looked, too, as though she was about to be lucky. Flicking the reins lightly, he seemed about to ride past.

But then suddenly he paused, drawing the reins in abruptly, as his gaze dropped to the ground beneath Liza's tree.

Liza squirmed inside. She knew what he'd spotted. She'd left her bag down there when she'd embarked on her climb.

Next moment, unhurriedly, the horseman was turning in her direction. 'Whoever you are, I suggest you come down and claim your property.' As he spoke, in a voice that was deep and richly masculine, he raised his eyes very slowly to look at her.

'You never know, there might be thieves and trespassers about.'

In that moment, as their eyes met, Liza felt a rush of emotion. She had known he would have a strong face, shrewd-eyed and intelligent, with probably more than a touch of arrogance about it, but she had not been prepared for its powerful chiselled beauty. Nor for the sheer sparkling magnetism of the long-lashed dark eyes.

Without putting it into words, as something shivered inside her, she knew in that instant that this man before her was the most bewitchingly attractive man she had ever met in her life.

She also knew that at that moment she must look a total idiot as she sat there, perched precariously in the fork of the tree, gaping down at him as though she were incapable of speech.

Quickly, she made an effort to pull herself together. 'I beg your pardon?' she stuttered, not really doing very well.

The sharp dark eyes narrowed. 'I said thieves and trespassers—though I'm assuming that, in fact, there's only one of you. Or am I wrong? Do you have someone else hiding up there with you?'

As he spoke, he shifted impatiently in the saddle, as though he might dismount and come up the tree after her to find out.

Liza felt a flicker of anxiety. 'No, there's no one here but me. And I wasn't really trespassing. I was just admiring the castle.'

'Were you, indeed?'

His tone was unimpressed, but at least, to Liza's relief, he hadn't dismounted. He continued to sit with magnificent arrogance in the saddle, regarding her with those unsettlingly magnetic dark eyes.

'Well, if you've done with admiring it,' he added, lifting one dark eyebrow, 'perhaps you'd like to come down now and explain yourself to me?'

'There's really nothing to explain.' Who was he? Liza asked herself, as, still clutching the tree-trunk, she glanced nervously towards the ground, wondering how on earth she was going to reach it. Did he actually have any right to question her like this?

But she knew she was in the wrong. She *had* been trespassing—even though it had all been in a good cause. And, anyway, she was in no position to argue with him.

She added apologetically, 'Look, I'm sorry I was trespassing, but I promise you I wasn't doing any harm.' As she spoke, she reached out tentatively with one foot for a toe-hold.

'You're an American. That accent...' The stranger on horseback eyed her as, very gingerly, she lowered herself an inch or two. 'It's definitely east coast. But not New York. A little further south. Baltimore, perhaps.'

'Close. In fact, very close.' Liza was impressed. She paused in her painfully slow descent. 'Actually,' she told him, smiling, 'I'm from Philadelphia.'

She'd been about to add that she wished she had his ear for accents. She'd been in England now for nearly a year, but she still wasn't much good at sorting out one accent from another!

But she didn't actually manage to say a single word of that. Before she could open her mouth, her interrogator was putting to her, 'So, is this what they teach you in Philadelphia? To go trespassing at will over other people's property?'

As his eyes ground into her, Liza felt a flare of annoyance. OK, so she'd been wrong, but she had apologised. This arrogant stranger really had no cause to go dishing out insults!

'I told you, all I was doing was admiring the castle.'

'Can't you read? Don't they teach you to read in Philadelphia?'

As Liza's eyes sparked at this second deliberate insult, his own eyes sparked back at her with a look of flinty warning.

'There are several large signs along the perimeter of this wood, warning people not to set foot beyond that perimeter. And warning them, too, that if they do they will be prosecuted.' His eyes challenged her. 'Didn't you see these signs?'

Liza nodded another apology. 'Yes, I did. I saw one of them. But I wanted to see the castle and——'

'And so you chose to ignore it.'

'It was only for five minutes! You can't see the castle from the road. And, anyway, I'm only a couple of yards inside the perimeter fence. I'm miles from the castle and I wasn't doing any harm!'

Liza's voice rose along with the frustration she was feeling. She seemed to have got stuck halfway down the wretched tree. Every time she glanced down the ground looked further away. And to add to her frustration, this infuriating man seemed absolutely hell-bent on giving her a hard time.

Her first impressions of him, she was fast deciding, had been mistaken. There was nothing even remotely attractive about him. Whoever he was, the only thing he was was maddening!

She glared down at him impotently from her leafy prison. 'I don't know why you're making such a fuss! I keep telling you all I was doing was admiring the castle!'

'So you do.' He eyed her, quite unmoved by her outburst. 'But why should I believe you when it's obvious you're lying? You weren't just admiring the castle, you were taking photographs. That looks suspiciously like a camera you're trying to hide.'

'I'm not trying to hide it!' With a bristle of indignation, Liza glanced down at the camera slung around her neck. 'And I wasn't taking photographs!' Though, to be honest, she had intended to. She'd promised Aunt Julia a couple of photographs of the castle. 'I haven't had time to take photographs!' she protested in frustration.

'So what else are you hiding?' The horseman ignored her protests. 'If you weren't hiding something, you wouldn't still be lurking up that tree.'

If she hadn't been so annoyed at him, Liza would have laughed at that. The only reason she was still up the tree was because she couldn't get down!

Still clutching at the tree-trunk, she cast an impatient look down at him. 'That's ridiculous. You're paranoid. I'm not hiding anything.'

'In that case, you won't mind if I find out who you are.'

As he spoke, as lithe as an acrobat, he leaned down from the saddle and, using his riding crop, scooped up her brown leather shoulder-bag. Then, straightening again, he made as though to look inside it.

'There must be something in here to tell me who you are.'

'How dare you? Get your hands off that!'

Sudden anger at the cheek of him sent a surge of adrenalin whipping through Liza. In an instant she had forgotten all about her fear of heights and was scrambling down the tree, slithering and sliding, to land with a bump on the grassy mound at the bottom. She straightened and darted towards him, trying to make a grab for her bag.

'Hand that bag over to me this instant!'

In response, he simply laughed and held the bag out of her reach. 'Yes, I thought that would get you down out of your tree!'

Close to, he was even more striking than he had been from the tree. He was about thirty-five, she guessed, and though his features weren't perfect—his nose wasn't quite straight and there was something a little lopsided about his mouth—it was still a devastatingly handsome face. Its beauty lay in the strength of its clean, sculpted lines and in the quick, sharp intelligence that shone from the dark eyes. There truly was something a little bewitching about this man.

But she had no desire to be bewitched, Liza reminded herself sharply. Shaking the feeling from her, she tilted her chin at him. 'I demand that you give me back my bag this instant.'

'Come and get it.'

With a tantalising smile that revealed a quick flash of perfect white teeth, the stranger slung the bag casually over his shoulder, holding the strap with his index finger.

'Come on,' he teased. 'Come and get it.' Then he paused, narrowing his eyes as his gaze travelled over her. 'You know, you look a lot better down on the ground than you did hanging on for dear life up in that tree.'

'I'm glad you think so.'

'No doubt about it.' He continued to examine her with bold dark eyes, taking in the head of pale auburn hair—currently more than a little ruffled!—that fell in thick soft waves to her shoulders, the wide green eyes, sensitive and intelligent, the short straight nose and the full-lipped mouth that at the moment was drawn into a tight angry line.

'Mind you, you'd look better without that frown between your brows. You shouldn't scowl like that, you know. What if the wind were to change?'

'I'm not interested in the wind. Just give me my bag back.'

He smiled again. 'I keep telling you, come and get it.'

Up until that moment Liza had been standing with her arm outstretched, doing her best to will him to hand over her bag. But as he continued to scrutinise her with that bold look in his eyes, his gaze drifting over her slim lithe figure, dressed in a skinny blue T-shirt and hip-skimming jeans, the brown leather belt that her boyfriend Elliott had given her emphasising the tiny dimensions of her waist, she felt a sudden need to fold her arms across her chest. The look of appreciation on his face was just a little too plain.

And what was more, she was suddenly acutely conscious of how close she was standing to him and the horse. And she wasn't fond of horses. They had too many hooves. And as for him...well, there was just something about the proximity of those leather riding boots and those hard-packed thighs encased in their perfect jodhpurs that was making the hairs on the back of her neck go all stiff. She swallowed and took a couple of discreet, but quick, steps back.

'So, who are you? Are you going to tell me, or do I have to find out for myself?' As he spoke, he twitched the strap of her shoulder-bag—a warning that, if he wanted to, he could find out for himself.

Liza smothered the urge to take another lunge at him. There was no way she could snatch the bag from his grip—unless she were to clamber bodily over the horse, and she'd already done enough of that sort of thing for one day!

'My name's Liza,' she told him, wondering why she hadn't added Blake. 'I'm from Philadelphia, as I've already told you. I'm twenty-four years old. I'm a physics teacher. And I've come to Yorkshire for a couple of weeks' holiday.' Impatiently, she flicked him a quick, sarcastic look. 'Is that enough or do you want more?'

'Much more.' There was another white flash of a smile. 'So far, we've only skimmed the surface.' As the horse shifted, he drew the reins tighter to settle it, then leaned back once more, casually, in the saddle. His eyes had never left Liza for an instant. They regarded her now with open interest.

'Liza... That's a pretty name. So, are you here on holiday with friends?'

'No, I'm not here with friends.' Good heavens, but he was curious! 'I'm here on my own, as a matter of fact.'

'On your own. That's unusual.' He regarded her suspiciously. 'You mean you've come all the way from Philadelphia to spend a fortnight in the north of England on your own?'

'Not exactly.' Liza pulled a face. 'If you really must know, for the past ten months or so I've been teaching at a school in London. Now that the school year's over and I've got some free time, I decided to spend a couple of weeks in Yorkshire.'

That was all perfectly true, though perhaps a trifle misleading. She'd made it sound as though her trip to Yorkshire had simply been a happy afterthought, when in fact it had been planned carefully right from the beginning. She had things to do here. Promises to keep for Aunt Julia. And the only reason she had come alone was because at the last minute her boyfriend Elliott had had to cancel.

Normally, she would have been quite happy to share this information. It was Liza's nature to be frank and open. But some instinct was warning her to keep her distance with this man—the same instinct that had stopped her from telling him her surname.

For some reason, clearly, he did not trust her. She might be wise, she sensed, to return the compliment.

Keeping her arms tightly folded across her chest, she frowned up at him and demanded, 'And who are you? I've told you who I am. Now it's your turn.'

'My turn?' In response, he shook his dark head. 'No, I don't think so. I haven't finished with you yet.'

'Are you something to do with the castle?' Liza pressed on, regardless. He wasn't the only one who could conduct an inquisition! 'They train and breed horses at the castle. The lady who runs the bed-and-breakfast where I'm staying told me.' She glanced at his horse, as though in support of her argument. 'I'm right, am I not? You do work for the castle? Is this what they pay you to do—to catch and torment trespassers?'

'As a matter of fact, they don't. This is strictly a sideline.' The stranger smiled down at her with arrogant amusement. 'Catching and tormenting trespassers is just something I do for entertainment.'

'Then I'm glad to have been able to provide you with some entertainment.' Liza flashed him a look of disapproval. 'And now, will you please give me my bag and let me go on my way?' Impatiently, she thrust out her hand again.

She might as well have not bothered. The handsome stranger shook his head. 'I'll give you your bag when I've finished with you,' he said.

As he spoke, the horse shifted again restlessly beneath him. He gave the reins a light snap, so that the horse swung round slightly, causing Liza to drop her arm and take another step back.

'You don't like horses, I see.' He smiled that arrogant, amused smile of his as the horse settled down, allowing him to loosen the reins again. 'But you shouldn't worry about Thunder. He won't harm you.'

'I don't expect he will, and I have nothing against him.'

Liza cast a doubtful glance at the large black stallion. Like all horses, in her small experience, there was just too much of him. Just too much dangerous, raw animal power. Though this arrogant stranger, she had to admit, seemed to have no trouble at all keeping all that power under control.

She cast him a glance of grudging admiration and was aware of a *frisson* of strange excitement whipping through her. When it came to dangerous raw animal power this man possessed ten times as much as any horse!

In the same instant that she thought it, Liza pushed the notion from her. It had caused a spurt inside her that was a little improper considering that she was already involved romantically with another man! Composing herself, she told the stranger, 'I'm a city girl, that's all. I just don't feel comfortable around horses and things like that.'

'So I see. So what brings you to Abbotsdale? There are rather a lot of horses and things like that here. A city girl like you would surely have been wiser to stay in London?'

Liza felt a flicker of annoyance. Who was he to tell her where she should or should not stay?

She raised impatient eyebrows. 'I wanted to see Yorkshire. I'd already seen London. Do you have any objections?'

'I haven't decided yet.' Again that insolent smile flashed, lighting the magnetic dark eyes with devilment. He leaned towards her slightly. 'So why did you come here? Here, precisely, to Abbotsdale? Was there any special reason?'

'I was told it's very beautiful.'

'It is very beautiful.' Just for an instant the warmth of pride touched his eyes. Then he raised dark eyebrows. 'But all of Yorkshire is beautiful. If it was just beauty you were after, you could have gone anywhere.'

Then he paused. 'I bet I know. I bet you're one of those Anglo-Americans who come over here looking for their roots?' He threw her a curious glance. 'I'm right, am I not?'

Liza nearly said yes. After all, it was more or less true. And it was a perfectly innocent and honourable reason. But something stopped her yes,

though she couldn't quite summon a no. She had
no desire to confide anything about herself to him,
but neither did she have any wish to lie.

'If you are, I can probably help you.' The dark
eyes continued to watch her. 'I know everything
there is to know about all the families around this
area. The Comptons, the Blakes, the Butlers, the
Gowers.' He paused and held her eye. 'Which one
are you?'

Liza glared at him, irritated. 'Why do you want
to know? Why don't you just give me my bag and
let me go?'

'Are you a Compton?'

'No.'

'A Butler?'

'No.'

'Then which family are you from? What's your
name?'

Liza shook her head. She really didn't want to
lie. All she wanted was to get her bag back and to
put an end to this ridiculous conversation. But, as
he sat there waiting for her answer, as though he
had every right in the world to be told, Liza's frustration and irritation suddenly got the better of her.

Looking straight at him, she lied, 'I'm a
Hardcastle.'

'There are no Hardcastles around here.'

Liza already knew that. She had a distant cousin
who was a Hardcastle and she'd already checked
in the local phone book!

For the first time during their encounter Liza
suddenly felt slightly one up, though at the same
time rather uncomfortable with that uncharacter-
istic lie. He forced me, she told herself, with his

impudent, prying questions. Besides, he hadn't revealed who he was, so why should she?

She regarded him levelly. 'I'm just a casual
tourist. I'd heard about the castle and I wanted to
see it. In fact, I was wondering if I might see inside.'
She slanted him a look. 'Do you think that might
be possible? If I had a word with the owners?' she
added.

'I doubt it. The castle's private. It's not open to
the public.'

Well, he would say that, wouldn't he? He was
hardly likely to help her!

'But I could speak to them. In fact, I already
intend to.' Liza threw him a defiant look. 'What's
their name?' she demanded, sensing he probably
wouldn't tell her.

He didn't. Instead, he put to her, 'You said you'd
heard about the castle. That surprises me. It's not
in any of the tourist guides. Perhaps you wouldn't
mind telling me how you came to hear about it?'

Liza paused for a moment. She could scarcely
tell him the truth. It would rather give the lie to her
claim to be a casual tourist. For, of course, she had
known about Abbotsdale Castle since her
childhood, and all about the wicked Hawkes family
who used to own it. And that was why she was here.
She was no casual tourist.

'Someone mentioned it to me,' she said vaguely,
hoping he would buy that. And it was true, she
reflected. Aunt Julia had told her.

But the stranger on horseback was clearly not
satisfied.

'Someone mentioned it to you?' he echoed dis-
believingly, that glint of suspicion in his eyes

growing stronger. 'Do you think you could possibly be a little more specific?'

'And why on earth should I be? What the devil's going on here?' Liza flashed him a look of angry frustration. 'You'd almost think you believed I was some kind of criminal!'

At that, a look crossed his eyes. 'Maybe you are,' he responded. 'It would certainly explain why you're being so secretive.' Then with a flick of his wrist, he unhooked her bag from his shoulder. 'Perhaps I should take a look in here, after all,' he added.

'You dare and I'll——'

As she spoke, Liza lunged towards him, arms flailing as she tried to grab the bag from him. But all that happened, as the horse whinnied and moved out of her path, was that she missed her footing and almost fell flat on her face.

But not quite. As she stumbled, as quick as lightning a hand had reached down and caught her firmly by the arm. And it continued to hold her as her intended victim chastised her, 'You shouldn't do things like that. You'll frighten Thunder.'

Liza didn't know what to say. She toyed with saying sorry. But she felt reluctant to say sorry and anyway she doubted she could have managed it. For all the breath seemed to have been knocked out of her at this unexpected development. Suddenly, her heart was pounding a little too rapidly for comfort.

The stranger was bending down towards her in the saddle, so that his face was very close to hers. And the dark eyes, Liza could see now, were flecked with grey and amber. They were extraordinary eyes, hauntingly beautiful, in whose depths seemed to flicker every conceivable passion. Never before had Liza looked into such eyes.

And they were sparking at her, teasing her, as he continued to hold her. 'What were you saying? What exactly were you about to do to me?'

Liza vaguely recalled that she'd been making some threat, but for the life of her she couldn't remember what it was. The warm scent of him that suddenly filled her nostrils, rich and heady, like some potent cocktail, seemed to be going straight to her head.

He drew her a little closer. 'Go on—what were you about to do?'

Forcing herself to breathe, Liza tried to snatch her hand away and was strangely dismayed when he continued to hold her.

'I'd report you, that's what I'd do, if you looked inside my bag!' Her green eyes glared at him as she said it, though her tone lacked the ferocity she had intended.

She tried again. 'In fact, I intend to report you anyway! When I go to ask permission to see round the castle, I'll tell them about you, whoever you are!'

'And what will you tell them?' The dark eyes danced and sparkled. He was clearly thoroughly enjoying infuriating her like this.

'I'll tell them you harassed me! I'll tell them you attacked me! I'll tell them you took my bag and wouldn't give it back!'

'Harassed you? Attacked you?' He laughed and sat back in the saddle, releasing his hold on her arm as he did so. 'Here, take your bag.' He tossed

it down to her. 'There, now you have no more cause
for complaint.'

Liza caught the bag and clutched it to her bosom
defensively, suddenly feeling just a little foolish. He
had been playing some game with her, she sensed.

She glared at him furiously. 'I'm still going to
report you! You're not going to get away with this,
you know!'

'You mean business, I see.'

'You'd better just bet I do! The first chance I
have, I'm going to the castle to report you!'

Sitting tall in the saddle, the stranger regarded
her for a moment. Then he smiled. 'Why wait? Why
not do it now?'

'What do you mean?' Liza frowned at him.
'What do you mean do it now?'

'I'll take you, if you like.'

'To the castle? To meet the owner?'

The stranger nodded. 'That's what you want, is
it not?'

'Yes, but——'

'But nothing.' He leaned forward and held his
hand out. 'Climb aboard. I'll take you now.'

'You mean climb up there with you?' Liza took
a step back. 'Up there with you on that horse? You
must be joking!'

'You'll be perfectly safe. I'll make sure you don't
fall off.' He paused and smiled that flickering, tantalising smile of his. 'Besides, you really oughtn't
to miss this opportunity. The owner isn't around a
lot.'

'And he's there now? And you think he'd see
me?'

'I believe he has some free time this afternoon.'

'I don't know...'

Still, Liza hesitated. Would it be wise, she was wondering, to climb up on to that huge beast with that infuriating man?

'OK, if you'd rather not...' He started to turn away. 'But, as I said, you may not get another chance.' He flicked the reins and prepared to ride off.

Liza stepped forward quickly then, squashing her doubts. 'OK. I'll come.' She bit her lip nervously. She had promised Great-aunt Julia she'd get inside the castle and maybe this would be her only chance to fix it.

She glanced up at the stranger. 'But please go slowly. Remember, I've never been on a horse before.'

'Don't worry, I'll look after you.' He drew the horse round and leaned down from the saddle, reaching out his hand towards her. 'You will never be in safer hands than these.'

Liza hoped he was right, but it was too late for doubts now. In one easy movement, as though she weighed nothing, he had swung her up into the saddle in front of him, one arm around her waist, the other holding the reins.

'By the way, did you know you had a large gash in the back of your jeans?'

At the amused note in his voice, Liza felt herself flush. She had entirely forgotten about the state of her jeans. She stared straight ahead, making no comment, as he added, 'But don't worry, I only caught a very quick glimpse.' His arm tightened around her waist. 'OK? Are you ready?' Then, as she nodded bravely, not really sure that she was and still burning with embarrassment to think of that tear in her jeans, he nudged the horse's sides with his knees.

Liza was clenched as tight as a fist as the horse began to move forward. This was a hundred times more terrifying than being stuck up a tree. And she was totally at the mercy of this man at her back whose arm she was clutching with every atom of her strength.

Then he proceeded to knock for six what little poise she had left.

In a calm tone, he observed, 'I think it's time I introduced myself. You asked me earlier who I was, but I never got round to telling you.' He paused just a fraction. 'My name is Richard Hawkes.'

In an instant Liza had forgotten all about the tear in her jeans. She had even forgotten how terrified she was to be on the horse. With eyes as wide as saucers, she half turned round to look at him.

'Hawkes, did you say?' she gulped. Surely she must be hearing things? Had she unwittingly put her life in the hands of one of the dreaded Hawkeses?

It was not a reassuring thought, but there was nothing she could do. It was a little too late to think of changing her mind now.

For suddenly, as though on wings, they were flying across the meadow, the wind tugging at her hair, the thunder of hooves in her ears.

And all Liza could do was close her eyes tight, hold on for dear life to his arm and pray.

CHAPTER TWO

'DID you really have to go quite so fast? Didn't you hear me when I asked you to keep your speed down?'

Liza was breathless by the time they reached the castle. She felt as though she'd just gone ten rounds with a whirlwind. Her cheeks were flushed and her legs felt quite shaky. As Richard lowered her to the ground, she gritted her teeth at him.

'That was just about the worst experience of my life!'

'I don't believe you.' In response, he simply smiled at her. 'Go on. Tell the truth. You rather enjoyed it.'

'You're the one who enjoyed it, you rotten sadist!'

With an effort Liza kept her expression steely—for the truth was she had found it rather exciting. Perched high on the powerful horse with the wind in her hair and Richard's arm wrapped securely round her waist, she'd felt very little fear and a huge sense of elation. She'd almost been sorry when they'd slowed down to a trot as they reached the cobbled courtyard at the back of the castle.

But she would die before she'd admit that to him! She pursed her lips at him. 'You might have killed me. I told you I'd never been on a horse before.'

He was slipping his feet from the stirrups and smiling down at her with an expression that was totally devoid of concern. 'You were in no danger. I promised you that and I meant it. Besides,' he added, getting ready to dismount, 'I knew you'd get the hang of it in no time. It's well known that all Hardcastles are natural riders.'

'Are they? I mean, we are?'

Liza was almost caught for a moment. It had briefly slipped her mind that she was supposed to be a Hardcastle. She was rather glad her cheeks were flushed already as she felt a blush rise up her throat.

Then she narrowed her eyes again. 'Well, I'm the exception. When it comes to travelling, this particular Hardcastle prefers things with four wheels to things with four legs.'

'Don't worry, you'd soon get the hang of it,' Richard told her. 'When it's in the blood it's in the blood.' With one supple movement, he had lowered himself to the ground. 'Once a Hardcastle, always a Hardcastle,' he added, looking into her face.

It was the first time Liza had seen him off the horse. She felt a jolt go through her as suddenly he was standing before her, all bristling, vibrant masculinity and even taller than she had expected. She wasn't exactly small, but he seemed to tower over her. He was at least half a head taller than Elliott, she thought admiringly, and far more muscularly built.

That quite inappropriate comparison caused a flash of guilt. He may be a little taller than Elliott, but her boyfriend was worth a dozen of him any day!

An instant later she found herself remembering what he'd told her at the start of their heart-

stopping ride. She raised her eyes to his and regarded him levelly. 'You told me back there your
name is Hawkes...'

As she paused, he nodded. 'That's right. Richard
Hawkes.'

Liza regarded him with curiosity. 'That's a coincidence. Wasn't Hawkes the name of the family
who used to own this place?'

'Yes, it was. You know a lot.' He raised dark
eyebrows. 'I thought you were supposed to be just
a casual tourist?'

'I am.'

She had slipped up, Liza told herself crossly.
Perhaps she oughtn't to have made that revealing
remark. But the truth was she was curious and the
only reason she was being cagey with him was because he seemed so suspicious of her. Did he really
think she'd been up to something up that tree?

But if he did, that was his problem. She would
soon put his boss right—about what she was really
here for, as well as the truth about her name. And,
in the meantime, she would continue to tell Richard
Hawkes nothing.

She smiled an innocent smile. 'The same person
who told me about the castle also told me all about
the Hawkeses.' Then she added, figuring, in for a
penny in for a pound, 'I understood the castle was
in their family for centuries, but that they all moved
away about twenty years ago and somebody
else took over the estate...' Her Aunt Julia, who
kept tabs on such things, had read that in
some magazine.

She shrugged. 'That's why I said it was a coincidence. You here, after all those years... A
Hawkes working at the castle...'

'If you say so.' Richard's expression had not
softened. His dark eyes bored into her as though
they would unearth all her secrets. And it was to
Liza's huge relief that precisely at that moment a
man in green wellies came striding across the
courtyard towards them.

He greeted Richard. 'Good ride, sir? I'll take
Thunder back to the stables for you and give him
a good rub down.'

'Thanks, Jim. Yes, I had an excellent ride.'
Richard handed over the reins to the man. 'Be sure
and give him an extra ration of oats tonight.'

'I will, sir.' With a smile the man took charge of
the horse and headed back across the courtyard.

Liza had listened to the brief exchange with
interest. Sir, indeed. She glanced at Richard.
Whatever position he held here, it was evidently a
fairly elevated one—not that she had for one
moment taken him for some stable-hand. He had
much too much poise and authority for that. He
was probably a manager of some description.

She turned to him. 'I realise you're probably very
busy—much too busy to waste time with me. So if
you could just take me to your boss and introduce
me, I'd be most grateful—and then you can get on
with your duties.'

That way, she was thinking, she would kill two
birds with one stone. Without further delay she
would meet the man she needed to talk to, and this
man, whom she wished she had never met in the

first place, would finally, mercifully, be out of her hair!

But as soon as she'd spoken, she wished she'd phrased her suggestion differently. Richard Hawkes was not a man to be told what to do. More than likely he would now proceed to do the very opposite.

But he simply smiled, though she suspected it was the smile of the viper. 'How thoughtful of you not to want to waste my time,' he told her. 'OK. Let's go. Just follow me.'

He led her on swift strides across the courtyard, his heels clicking a sharp tattoo against the cobbles. And as Liza hurried after him, she took the opportunity to reach a hand quickly behind her to check the state of her jeans.

Her heart sank a little. He hadn't been joking. It really did feel like a rather large gash. Oh, well, she decided, I'll just have to make sure I keep my back turned, and in emergencies use my bag as camouflage!

But the state of her jeans couldn't dampen her enthusiasm as she hurried behind him across the ancient cobblestones. She could scarcely believe it was really happening. She was actually about to take her first step inside the castle!

Not very far inside, though. She was led through a stone porch, then up a couple of steps and into a small tiled hallway. Then Richard was pushing open a door, old and heavy-looking, and leading her into the room beyond.

'Wait here,' he told her. 'I'll only be a moment.' Then, with a quick, amused smile, he turned on his heel and left her.

Before she did anything else, Liza glanced round her. The room where he had left her was small, but it was perfect. It was beautifully proportioned, with a high beamed ceiling and wonderful carved oak-panelled walls.

Liza had seen rooms like this in movies, but never in real life. It was a style people often copied, but rarely managed to get quite right. But this was right. And no wonder, it was the original. It even smelled right. It smelled deliciously of old polish and history.

She sank into a tapestry armchair and sighed with pleasure, admiring the heavy-framed oil paintings on the walls, the beautiful, carefully preserved antiques, the exquisite Aubusson rug on the floor.

'Oh, Aunt Julia,' she whispered, 'how I wish you could be here! This would absolutely knock you out!'

At the thought of her great-aunt a smile touched Liza's eyes. It was Aunt Julia who had raised her since she was seven years old, after her parents and her brother had been killed in a road accident. And it was Aunt Julia who had filled her childhood with wonderful stories, most of them centring around Abbotsdale Castle.

The stories had been passed down from Aunt Julia's own great-grandmother, who for a while had been a servant in Abbotsdale Castle before finally fleeing from Yorkshire with her husband to begin a new life in the promised land of America.

'They were driven from England,' Aunt Julia had often told her, 'by the wicked Hawkes family who'd been the Blakes' enemies for centuries.' And she would frown and shudder as she embellished her story. 'Those Hawkeses were the scourge of us poor Blakes.'

In all the years since the Blakes had settled in Philadelphia none of them had ever recrossed the Atlantic. So when Liza landed her one-year exchange post in London the entire family had been over the moon.

And none more so than Aunt Julia.

'Promise you'll visit Yorkshire,' she'd beseeched Liza earnestly. 'And try to visit Abbotsdale and come back and tell me all about it.'

'I will,' Liza had vowed. 'I'll go to Abbotsdale and I'll visit the castle and I'll take masses of photographs. When you see what I bring back, you'll feel as though you've been there yourself!'

Liza smiled to remember the way her aunt's eyes had shone. 'If you can, try to do me a very special favour,' she'd asked Liza. 'Try to take some pictures of the ballroom at the castle. My great-grandmother always said it was a magical place. More than anything, that's what I'd love you to bring back pictures of.'

So, that was Liza's mission and she was determined to accomplish it. That was why she was prepared to go clambering up trees and risking her life on the back of a horse! She adored the old lady and there was nothing she wouldn't do for her. Come hell or high water, she planned to get these pictures!

She frowned now and glanced at the big oak door that Richard Hawkes had disappeared through just a moment ago. That was a turn-up for the books—that one of the first people she should bump into was an infuriating tyrant by the name of Hawkes!

Aunt Julia would be highly amused when she told her!

Of course, it was just a coincidence. Hawkes was a common enough name—she'd found at least a score of them listed in the local phone book—and this particular Hawkes tyrant was unlikely to be related to those other Hawkes tyrants of all those years ago. As soon as she'd thought about it rationally, Liza had realised that. Though it had definitely given her a bit of a start when Richard Hawkes had told her his name. She'd felt plunged back into the murky mists of history.

She sat back in the tapestry armchair. No, this particular Hawkes was very much a demon of the present—and one she sincerely hoped that after today she might be spared the unpleasantness of having any more dealings with.

And it seemed quite likely that she would be spared. He was merely an employee. Once she'd been introduced to his boss, the owner of the castle, she could just forget that she'd ever had the misfortune to lay eyes on him.

She glanced at her watch. 'I'll only be a moment,' he had told her, though the promise had been accompanied by a quick, amused smile that had warned her not to hold her breath. Keeping her waiting would appeal to him. In fact, he might well go further. It was perfectly conceivable that right at this moment he was putting in a bad word for her and advising his boss not to see her. She sensed he'd love to send her off empty-handed.

Well, he wouldn't succeed. Liza glanced round her. Now that she'd got this far, nothing was going to stop her. With or without his assistance, she wouldn't be leaving the castle until she'd come face to face with its owner.

'Still waiting, I see.'

Suddenly, the door had opened and Richard Hawkes was stepping into the room.

He smiled at her, that irritatingly self-assured smile. 'I was a little longer than I intended. I hope you weren't bored?'

'Not bored at all.' Liza rose to her feet, struggling to smother the electric sensation that had shot through her at the sight of him walking through the door.

He was still dressed as before, in riding boots and jodhpurs and a dark green roll-neck cashmere sweater. But as he had stepped into the room, a shaft of sunlight from the window had momentarily fallen across him like a spotlight. The effect had been quite startlingly dramatic.

Those strong, arresting features of his had seemed even more arresting than ever, and the dark hair, which flopped down engagingly over his forehead, had seemed to glisten like polished jet.

Liza found herself returning cautiously to her original opinion. He *was* a most beguilingly attractive man. Though he was not her type. Elliott was her type. Richard Hawkes' attractiveness resided solely in his good looks. It most definitely did not extend to his character!

She threw him as level a look as she could manage, for her heart was still rushing strangely inside her. 'I was admiring the décor,' she told him in a cool tone. 'This really is a lovely room.'

'Yes, it is. But then the castle has many lovely rooms.' He smiled a knowing smile, amused and taunting. 'However, no doubt you were already aware of that? As we've established, you know quite a lot about the place.'

'Yes, I was told the castle had many lovely rooms.' Liza looked back at him with a flicker of impatience. How long did he intend standing there making irritating conversation? She raised a questioning eyebrow. 'So?' she demanded. 'Did you speak to your boss? Is he going to see me?'

Richard met her gaze. He was still smiling with amusement. 'Yes, he'll see you. He's prepared to give you a few minutes.'

Then, throwing her, he proceeded to seat himself in a nearby armchair.

Liza blinked at him. 'Excuse me? What do you mean?' she protested. 'Are you telling me he's coming here?' She remained standing where she was, as he sat back in his chair and stretched out his booted feet in front of him. 'If he is, you needn't wait. I can see him alone. There's really no need for you to stay.'

'I'm afraid there is.' Richard simply made himself more comfortable. 'In fact, I'm afraid it's essential that I stay. Otherwise, there will be no meeting.'

'Why?' Liza peered at him, trying to hide her annoyance. What the devil was going on?

And then he surprised her. He waved to the tapestry chair, where up until a couple of minutes ago she'd been sitting. 'Make yourself comfortable,' he invited her. 'And let's get on with our meeting.'

'*Our* meeting? What do you mean *our* meeting?'

'Just that, my dear Miss Hardcastle. I'm the man you've come to see.'

'*You*?'

Just for a moment Liza thought he must be joking. But, as she looked into his face, although he was still smiling, she could see that, alas, he was deadly serious.

She sank with dismay into the tapestry armchair. 'You mean *you're* the owner of the castle?'

'Lock, stock and barrel.' Richard's smile had grown wider. 'Every stick and stone of it belongs to me.'

So, she'd been wrong, Liza observed to herself. It would appear that, after all, he really was a descendant of the original Hawkes family. That made her twice as angry now at the way he had tricked her.

'Why didn't you tell me, right from the beginning?' she demanded angrily. 'Why did you pretend you only worked here? Why all that pantomime about taking me to meet your boss?'

'I suspect you mightn't have believed me if I'd told you who I was.' Richard looked back at her, dark eyes unrepentant. 'And, besides, if you cast your mind back,' he accused her, 'it was you who assumed I only worked here.'

'I thought the owner would be much older. That was why I assumed that.' And he was right; almost certainly she wouldn't have believed him. All the same, she accused him back, 'I suppose you enjoy misleading people?' Knowing his family history, she had no doubt that he did! 'Is this another of the ways you entertain yourself—giving innocent people the runaround and wasting their time?'

'Innocent?' Richard smiled at that. 'I think you're forgetting. You, Miss Hardcastle, are a trespasser. That scarcely entitles you to call yourself innocent.'

Each time he called her Miss Hardcastle, Liza felt a quick dart inside her. It was a mixture of guilt at the lie she had told him and a growing sense of certainty that she'd done the right thing. For with every second that passed she was growing surer and surer that the less Richard Hawkes knew about her and her mission, the better.

If he knew what she was after and how important it was to her, he would only make a point of standing in her way.

She glared at him now. 'Is that why you lured me here? So that you can in some way punish me for climbing up your wretched tree?'

'Why, don't you think I'd be justified in punishing you?'

As the dark eyes fixed her, Liza felt a flutter of anxiety. She hadn't been serious when she'd suggested that was his motive, but now all at once she wasn't so certain. She found herself glancing a little nervously past his shoulder and calculating how quickly she could make it to the door.

But he was saying, 'However, punishment was not what I had in mind.' Which was just as well, Liza decided. She could never have beaten him to the door. With those long legs of his he could probably make it in two strides!

Relieved at least on that point, she swivelled her dark eyes back to look at him. 'So, why did you lure me here?' she wanted to know.

Richard Hawkes smiled. 'I lured you here, Miss Hardcastle, for an altogether different reason. As it happens, I have a proposition to make.'

'A proposition?' Liza raised a pair of sceptical eyebrows. 'What sort of proposition could you possibly have in mind that I would be likely to consider?'

None, she answered privately to herself.

Unperturbed by her scepticism, Richard sat back in his seat, his dark eyes roving unhurriedly over her face, then pausing to admire the fall of pale auburn hair.

'I seem to remember that you said you were a teacher. A teacher of physics, if I remember right.'

Liza nodded, still sceptical. 'Yes, that's what I said.' She wished he would stop looking at her that way, his eyes moving all over her like intimate, caressing fingers. It was causing her scalp to prickle most uncomfortably.

He smiled. 'That's good. It means at least you have some skills. It means you can probably write and almost certainly add up.'

Damned cheek! Liza glared at him. 'Actually, it means a little more. It means I also know the difference between a test tube and a bunsen burner.'

Her burst of sarcasm simply amused him. 'I expect you do, Miss Hardcastle,' he acknowledged. 'However, I'm afraid such specialised scientific knowledge won't be called for in the little scenario I have in mind.'

'And what little scenario might that be?' Liza felt a twinge of apprehension. What the devil was he about to try and talk her into?

But he did not answer her question immediately. Instead, looping one arm casually over the back of his chair, he observed, narrowing his eyes at her,

'Physics. That's a strange choice. Whatever made you go into physics?'

'I don't know what's so strange about it.'

Liza found herself pausing, her attention momentarily distracted by the way his green sweater was suddenly stretched over the powerful muscles of his chest. He really was rather magnificently built.

Then she tore her eyes away, furious at herself. Was she losing her wits that she could react to him this way?

A little testily, she said, 'I suppose you think that women teachers should stick to subjects like English literature and needlework?'

'If that's what they want to stick to.' Richard tossed off her accusation with an unconcerned shrug of his shapely shoulders. 'I'm a great believer in people doing whatever job suits them.'

'Or whatever suits their sex.'

Liza fixed him with a disapproving look, yet aware of a subtle sense of satisfaction. He was a male chauvinist, that was clear. She eyed the taut lines of his chest again, but this time with distaste, not admiration. He was one of those ghastly, unbearable macho men who like women to be doormats who know their place. She'd never had any trouble despising men like that.

In a disdainful tone, she added, 'I'm sorry if it bothers you, but I don't happen to believe in sex-based boundaries when it comes to things like careers.'

'You think women should be navvies?' He leaned back and smiled provocatively. 'Perhaps you think they should take up pickaxes and go down mines?'

Liza thinned her lips at him. Trust him to go to extremes! 'On the whole, no, I don't,' she conceded in a caustic tone. Then she added, 'Though, I've no doubt, there are some women around who would be perfectly capable of doing jobs like that.'

'If there are, good luck to them. I'd be the last one to stop them.' Richard smiled. 'Though, quite frankly, I think they'd be better off teaching physics.'

'Or even better still, English literature or needlework.'

'If that was what suited them.' He paused for a moment. Then he surprised her. 'Why are you so touchy?' he wanted to know.

'I'm not touchy.'

'Oh, yes, you are. You jumped straight to the wrong conclusion. When I said, about physics, that I thought it was a strange choice, you immediately assumed I meant a strange choice for a woman.'

'Well, that was what you meant, wasn't it?'

'As a matter of fact, it wasn't. What I meant was that it struck me as a strange choice for you.'

'For me? Why would you think that? You don't even know me.'

Liza was trying to sound clipped and cool and in control, but there he was again, looking across at her in that intense, dissecting way he had, making the prickles in her scalp spread almost halfway down her spine. He had this way of looking at her that felt almost like he was touching her.

It wasn't a lewd look. It wasn't offensive. But it was oddly intimate, as though he could see inside her. And she found the intimacy of it disconcerting. No wonder she was acting a trifle touchy!

And now, he proceeded to disconcert her further.

'You're right, I don't really know you,' he admitted. 'But there are three things I happen to be a very good judge of. Horses, wine...' He paused. 'And women.'

As Liza scowled at that, he smiled amusedly and continued, 'And my judgement of you is that you're the type of young woman who enjoys dealing with people. You like to get out there and mingle, not lock yourself in a lab with a bunch of test tubes and bunsen burners.'

'I don't mind lab work.'

'But you enjoy teaching more.'

'I enjoy all of my job.'

But he was right, she conceded privately. What she loved about her job was communicating with her students. She was a teacher first and a scientist second. Sometimes she thought she'd be happy teaching anything!

Still, she kept that to herself. He'd judged her too accurately for comfort! Straightening in her seat, she pointed out to him in a clipped tone, 'We appear to have strayed from the subject under discussion. I'm still waiting to hear about this proposition you were going to put to me.' She smiled sarcastically. 'It's academic, of course. I can't see me being even remotely interested in any proposition of yours.'

He must have moved his foot as she was speaking. Something, definitely, must have distracted her. For, to her dismay, as she came to the end of her sentence, Liza found that her eyes had drifted down to his shiny boots, then along the length of his muscular legs to rest on his lean, taut thighs.

Fighting a flush of embarrassment, she snatched her gaze away. 'Not in any proposition I can even remotely think of,' she emphasised.

'I think you're wrong about that.' Richard held her gaze for a moment, making it even harder for her to fight back her blush. 'But I'll put you out of your misery. I'll tell you what it is.' He leaned towards her. 'I want you to come and work for me as my personal assistant.'

'Work for you? That's ridiculous! I'm not looking for a job! I'm here on holiday. I'll be going back to London in a couple of weeks!'

'A couple of weeks, until the end of July, are all I want you for. I'm afraid my previous PA has rather left me in the lurch and the new girl I've found can't start until August. So I rather desperately need someone to fill in. Someone who's bright enough to turn her hand to anything, whether it's working in the office or outdoors with the horses...'

'Well, that's definitely not me, even if I were looking for a job! I might be able to manage the office work, but nothing could persuade me to work with horses!'

Richard looked into her eyes as though he knew better. Then he smiled. 'Look on the bright side. You'll also be working with me.'

Then he continued, 'And if you accept, there'll be a room for you at the castle, and of course you'll more or less have the free run of the estate.'

He smiled a knowing smile. 'We have a very strict rule here. The only people who are allowed within the boundaries of the estate are myself, my friends and the people who work here. Everyone else who sets foot inside is considered a trespasser. And I'm afraid I don't make any exceptions.' He looked at her. 'You said you wanted to see inside the castle, so here you are... This is your chance.'

'You mean you won't allow me inside otherwise?'

He shook his head. 'I'm afraid not.'

'But I just want a quick look round. An hour or so would do. I don't see why it should be necessary for me to take a job and move in.'

'That's the deal, I'm afraid.' Richard began to rise to his feet, slipping his hands into the pockets of his jodhpurs. 'You either accept the deal or else you stay away from the castle.'

There was a steely note in his voice, a note of warning. If she turned down the deal and was caught trespassing again, she could bank on it that she wouldn't be let off lightly. 'Trespassers will be prosecuted,' the sign had warned. It would be a police matter, no doubt about it, if she was ever caught again.

Liza sighed. And she would never get inside the castle, nor be able to keep all the promises she'd made Aunt Julia.

He was waiting for her answer. 'Well, is it yes or is it no?'

Liza hesitated a moment longer, but she knew she was trapped. As much as she wanted to, how could she possibly say no?

She rose to her feet to face him. 'OK,' she assented. 'It looks as though I don't have much choice.'

Richard did not look surprised. In fact it was rather irritating the way he smiled as though he had never for one moment doubted her answer.

But as Liza looked into his face, she was making herself a promise. He was mad if he thought she'd stay on for the whole two weeks. She would stay only for just as long as she absolutely had to in order to get the photographs she needed for Aunt Julia. And then she would be off out of here like a shot!

He had taken a step towards her. 'Don't think of getting up to anything,' he warned her, almost as though he could see inside her head. 'You see, I don't believe for one moment that you're just a casual tourist... So, when I say that you and I are going to be working together, what I mean, my dear Miss Hardcastle, is that we'll be working so closely that people are going to mistake us for Siamese twins.'

He reached up unexpectedly to catch her chin with his fingers. 'For the entire two weeks I'm going to be stuck to you like a limpet. You won't be able to make a single move that I won't know about.'

'Really?' Liza looked back at him with eyes of green fire. You're wrong! she thought fiercely. I'll be gone before you even know it. You'll be lucky if you manage to stick to me for more than five minutes!

And for a moment as they stood there, facing one another, the air all around them seemed to crackle. The gloves were off. The battle had begun.

CHAPTER THREE

'It was incredible! I could scarcely believe it was happening! One minute he had me galloping across the fields on this crazy horse and the next he was demanding that I go and work for him! I've never met such a madman in my life!'

Liza was on the phone to Elliott, back at her bed-and-breakfast, telling him about her encounter with Richard Hawkes that afternoon.

'Anyway, I agreed to take the job,' she continued, 'just so I can get into the castle. But I won't be staying long. Just as soon as I've got what I want, I'll cut my holiday short and get on the first train back to London.' She laughed. 'Expect me back by the end of the week at the latest.'

'Nothing would please me more.' But Elliott sounded concerned. 'Hey, are you sure it's wise to go and work for this man? He really does sound like a bit of a madman to me.'

Liza was sitting cross-legged on the patchwork quilt on her bed, dressed in her robe, her hair still wet from the shower. 'Oh, he's mad, all right, but I don't think he's dangerous. He's just as arrogant as they come and hopelessly infuriating!'

'Well, if you think you're doing the right thing...'

'I have no choice, Elliott. It's the only way I can get inside the castle. And, like I said, I won't be sticking around for long. I'll just take the photographs for Aunt Julia and then I'll be gone.'

'OK, but take care and phone me again in a couple of days, just to let me know how it's going.'

After agreeing to his demands and blowing him a kiss down the phone, Liza laid down the receiver and smiled to herself. Thank heavens for Elliott, she was thinking. An oasis of sanity in all this madness!

She lay back on the bed and gazed up at the ceiling. Elliott had been keen to come with her on her trip to Yorkshire and he'd been disappointed when work commitments had made that impossible, though he'd promised to come up and spend at least one weekend with her.

Liza had been disappointed, too. She and Elliott had grown close during the six months or so they'd been together. It would have been nice to share her Yorkshire experience with him.

She'd met Elliott through a mutual friend in London. Like her, he was an American—a born and bred New Yorker—and currently he was working for a bank in the City. And they'd hit it off instantly. They had so much in common. They both loved art galleries and concerts and restaurants, and they'd had a great time getting to know London together. And getting to know each other, too.

Liza smiled and sat up, reaching for the towel on the nearby chair, and gave her wet hair a vigorous rub. She had a feeling that in the future they'd be getting to know each other even better. Like her, Elliott was due to return to the States in September, and they'd already talked about making regular trips between Philadelphia and New York!

But that was the future. She still had the present
to contend with. The present in the shape of the
abominable Richard Hawkes!

She paused for a moment and glanced with a wry
smile at the chair where her newly darned jeans lay
folded. The damage, once she'd had a look at it,
hadn't been so bad, she'd discovered. A couple of
stitches had soon put it right. In spite of his teasing,
Richard had probably glimpsed nothing as he lifted
her up on to the horse!

That thought made her heart lurch. The horse.
That ride. That amazing wild gallop across the
meadow.

But she pushed the thought from her and got up
from the bed, glancing at her watch and giving her
hair another rub. It was time she dried her hair off
and thought about getting some sleep. She had an
early start tomorrow.

Less than fifteen minutes later she was climbing
into bed, grumbling to herself as she set the alarm.
This was supposed to be a holiday and look what
had happened! She'd ended up working for that
wretched man! The next few days, until she could
escape, were going to be an abomination. Suddenly,
she couldn't wait to get back to Elliott.

But her last thoughts that night were not of
Elliott. As she switched off the light, she found
herself glancing at her jeans again. And again she
was remembering that wild gallop across the
meadow.

And no matter how hard she tried to push it from
her mind and think of other things as she curled
up beneath the covers, memories of that ride with

Richard just kept intruding, poking at her consciousness like insistent jabbing fingers.

And as she drifted off to sleep she could feel his arm around her and his hard chest pressing against her back, as they flew as though on wings together on horseback, the wind tugging at her hair, the blood leaping in her veins.

Liza arrived at the castle, wearing a scowl and carrying her suitcase, shortly after eight-thirty, as arranged.

Richard had told her to meet him in the office—which was in the south wing, near the rear courtyard—and that was where she was headed now. Some holiday! she was thinking. Some relaxation! She hadn't stopped cursing Richard since the alarm had gone off at seven o'clock.

Needless to say, he was waiting for her. As she pushed the door open, he glanced up at her from behind a large oak desk.

'You're looking bright and cheerful this morning.' He regarded her scowling face with a smile of amusement. 'That's what I like to see. Someone who's enthusiastic about their work.'

Liza plonked down her case. 'Oh, I'm ecstatic,' she shot back at him. 'I just can't wait to get down to the stables and start mucking out the horses.'

'All in good time. I'm saving that treat till later.' Tossing down his pen, he stood up and surveyed her. 'I see you took my advice to dress sensibly,' he observed. His eyes flitted over her tall, slim figure, dressed in a yellow cotton sweatshirt, trainers and jeans, then came up to focus once more on her face.

'I hope you've mended those jeans of yours, by the way.' His eyes danced with devilment as he said it. 'I wouldn't want you scandalising my staff.'

Liza glared at him and deliberately ignored that remark, though she had felt a faint flush touch her cheeks momentarily. 'Since I'm here, why don't we get down to business?' she suggested tightly. Anything would be better than bandying words with him!

He was unfazed by her sharpness. He simply continued to smile at her in that irritatingly arrogant way he had. He would be a hard man to get the better of, Liza found herself thinking. One had the feeling he was constantly at least five jumps ahead. That he knew what you were thinking before you'd even thought it yourself.

I shall have to play him very cautiously, she warned herself, if I'm to get what I want and make a speedy escape.

He had come round to the front of the desk and was leaning against it, a tall, muscular figure dressed in jeans like herself—brown boots and a grey shirt with the sleeves rolled back to the elbows.

'OK,' he said, folding his strong arms across his chest. 'Let's do as you say. Let's get down to business.'

Half an hour later, Liza was beginning to realise exactly what Richard meant by business, and it was all rather more impressive than she had expected. This wasn't just some two-horse outfit he was running, some backwoods rich man's indulgent hobby. What he had here was a slick, highly professional operation.

'At the moment we have twenty horses in our training stables. Apart from Thunder, who's mine, they all belong to clients.' He smiled a mischievous smile at her. 'You remember Thunder? He's the black stallion who gave you your taste for riding.'

Then, as she grimaced, suppressing an uncomfortable flutter of remembrance, he stabbed a button on the computer keyboard. 'All the relevant details of the horses are here. Owners' names, horses' histories, bloodlines and training records.' He stabbed another button. 'Here are all the coming season's races with details of the horses we plan to enter in them.' He stabbed again. 'Veterinary records.' Another stab. 'Prize money.' Stab. 'A list of jockeys.' Stab. 'Accounts for livery.'

He turned to glance at her. 'And, of course, on the breeding side we have a whole set of corresponding data.' He continued to fix her faintly shell-shocked face. 'So. Do you think you've got the hang of it?'

Liza blinked at him. 'You must be joking! You don't seriously expect me to master all this?'

'Not master it. Just get a working knowledge of what it's all about. That shouldn't be too hard for a smart girl like you.'

'Maybe I'm not that smart. At least, not when it comes to horses. I know they've got four legs, but that's just about all I know about them!'

'In that case, you're going to have to make a bit of an effort, aren't you?' His tone was light, but with a steely edge to it. It was clear he expected her to take her job seriously. She wouldn't get away with lame excuses. 'Otherwise, we're going to have problems, aren't we?'

Liza looked into his face with its amber- and grey-flecked eyes that seemed to have this ability to look right down inside her. He knew as well as she did that she was smart enough to do the job right, that she could easily learn if she put her mind to it—and that if she failed it would only be out of sheer bloody-mindedness, because she hated this arrangement he'd tricked her into.

Their eyes met and held for a moment, like antlers locked in combat. And silently, hating him with every bone and fibre, Liza re-pledged her promise to herself that her stay here would be brief. She'd be out of here just as fast as she could arrange it!

It was at that moment that the office door suddenly opened and in walked a bright-eyed, smiling young woman.

'Ah, Penny, there you are.' Richard turned round to greet her, his expression transformed, not a harsh look in sight. 'This is Liza. She's going to be filling in for us for a couple of weeks.'

Then he turned to Liza. 'Penny runs the office. If you have any problems, I'm sure she'll be able to help you. But in the meantime...' He paused and glanced at Liza's suitcase by the door. 'Penny will take you to meet Mrs Donnelly, my housekeeper. She can tell you which room she's prepared for you. But be back here in fifteen minutes.' He smiled sadistically. 'Next is the bit you've really been looking forward to. I'm going to introduce you to the horses.'

Well, at least there's one person in this outfit I can relate to, Liza decided, as she followed Penny through the castle corridors. For she had taken a liking to the other girl immediately. She and Penny, she felt instinctively, could be friends.

Though it was quite clear they didn't share the same views on some things!

'You'll love it here,' Penny told her, as they made their way towards the castle kitchens. 'Mr Hawkes is a good boss. Demanding, but fair. Everyone who works for him just adores him.'

I'll be the exception to that, Liza decided, groaning inwardly. She changed the subject slightly. 'He certainly has a lovely place.'

For on their short trek through the maze of corridors, she had rapidly come to realise that Abbotsdale Castle was an absolute gem. In her mind's eye she had already shot a couple of rolls of film to take back to Philadelphia to show to Aunt Julia!

Another gem, she soon discovered, was Mrs Donnelly, the roly-poly Irish housekeeper. So, already, there were two people she'd rather taken to. It was comforting to know that Richard was in the minority!

'I've prepared the little guest-room,' Mrs Donnelly told Liza. 'It's got a lovely view of the gardens. I hope you like it.'

The little guest-room, Liza reflected a couple of minutes later, as Penny stepped ahead of her and flung the door open, would be very difficult not to like. It was a glorious room, decorated in a rich rose colour and at least twice the size of the room she'd just checked out of at the bed-and-breakfast.

She grinned at Penny. 'Yes, I reckon I can put up with this!'

And just for the tiniest, most fleeting of moments she almost wished she were going to be staying longer. The little guest-room was positively the loveliest bedroom she'd ever seen.

But an instant later she was bumping back down to earth again.

Penny was glancing at her watch. 'We'd better be getting back. We don't want to keep Mr Hawkes waiting.'

'Definitely not.'

Liza pulled a face inwardly. How could she, even fleetingly, have thought about prolonging her agony? How could she have forgotten about Richard Hawkes?

Richard was waiting for her outside the office, at the wheel of a dark green Range Rover.

'Hop in,' he told her. 'We're going for a short ride.'

Liza climbed in beside him. I hope it *is* short, she was thinking. Somehow, she didn't fancy being cooped up inside the car with him. His bare brown arm, as he shifted the gearstick, was just a little too muscular and a little too close to her leg. She found it hard to keep her eyes off it and even harder to keep her leg still, though there was really no danger of his arm brushing against her.

It's all in my mind, she thought, glancing away swiftly. But the trouble was she knew what that strong brown arm felt like. It was the same arm that had been wrapped round her as they'd galloped across the meadow. The memory of its steely hard strength made her shiver.

But, thank heavens, in a few minutes they were drawing up outside the stables. Almost before he'd pulled on the handbrake, Liza was pushing open the door and jumping down, thankful to put a distance between them.

'So, this is what a stables looks like. How very interesting.' She cast a far from interested glance around her, rather hoping he hadn't noticed her crazy behaviour in the car.

Richard simply smiled as he slammed shut the driver's door and proceeded to lead her towards the stable buildings. 'It gets even more interesting when you get closer,' he promised her.

That was debatable. Forty minutes later Liza was thinking she'd seen enough of horses to last her a lifetime—though Richard's enthusiasm for his work and his obvious attachment to all his animals she had at times found rather touching. He clearly cared a great deal for all of them, especially Thunder.

He'd insisted on introducing her to each and every one of them—as well as to Jim, the stable manager, the man in green wellies she'd met briefly yesterday, and to all the stable lads and girls. And he'd also insisted on telling her a bit of each animal's history.

'I don't know why you're bothering,' Liza had complained at one point. 'I can see that they come in all sorts of different sizes and colours, but really they're all the same to me.'

'No, they're all different. Each has his or her own personality.' Richard had slanted her a glance designed to needle her. 'You'll discover that for yourself once you've been around them long enough.'

'I doubt it.' She'd flicked a look back at him. I won't be around them long enough, she'd silently promised herself. Then, out loud, she'd added with a deliberately flippant smile, 'But it doesn't really matter, does it? As long as I know which end to feed the oats to.'

Richard shook his head. 'You'll soon know a great deal more than that. In fact, by the time you leave Abbotsdale, I guarantee you'll have become something of an expert.'

Liza pulled a face. 'Lucky me,' she taunted. 'That's going to come in really handy when I get back to Philadelphia. My friends are going to be incredibly impressed.'

She tossed her head scoffingly and narrowed her eyes at him. 'When I tell them all about my visits to the Royal Opera House and the Tower of London, I'll also make sure to tell them that I'm now an expert on horses!'

'Is that all you care about?' Richard had turned more fully to face her. 'Is that what it's all about for you? Impressing your friends?'

Liza was taken aback by this unexpected accusation. She took a moment to reply. Then she tilted her chin at him. 'Like you, you mean, with all your fine horses? Is this how you impress your friends?'

'I don't need to impress my friends. They already know who I am.'

And so do mine, Liza almost replied, but she bit the words back. Why should she feel the need to justify herself to him? She didn't give a tinker's damn what he thought of her!

So, instead, she simply glared at him. 'I'm surprised you have any friends!'

That was the end of that exchange. Richard had simply shrugged off her little dig, not put out by it in the slightest. Then they had left the stables and, as though nothing had happened, he had gone on to show her the nearby paddock and the adjoining practice track where all the horses received their training.

But though Liza tried to put the incident behind her, she was aware that it had left her feeling distinctly ruffled. She'd only made that stupid remark about the Royal Opera House and the Tower of London to emphasise the gulf between them. Wanting to impress her friends just didn't come into it. And it irked her that he had managed to twist it to her disadvantage.

But what irked her more was that she was irked in the first place! She ought to be able to shrug off his insults the way he shrugged off hers. His opinion of her was the last thing she ought to care about.

At last, he was leading her back to the Range Rover.

'We'll go back to the office now. I have to make a couple of phone calls.' Richard glanced at his watch. 'But we have a bit of time. We'll go back the long way and I can show you some of the countryside.'

'Don't bother on my account.' As Liza looked back at him, she was glad to observe that she no longer felt ruffled. She met his gaze levelly. 'I'm a townie, remember? I like concrete and asphalt, not meadows and trees.'

'All the more reason to educate you.' He paid as much heed as she'd expected he would, as he pulled open the driver's door and climbed inside. 'This can be your first lesson in rural appreciation.'

Overbearing pig! As she climbed in beside him and they headed out on to the open road that circled the estate, Liza resigned herself to her coming ordeal and just hoped very hard that it might be brief.

She had nothing in the slightest against trees and meadows. In fact, in a way, she rather liked them. But she had a great deal against being given lessons in rural appreciation by Richard. And, like before, she wasn't too crazy about being cooped up with him in the car. Remembering how it had affected her last time, she kept her eyes fixed straight ahead and didn't glance down at the brown hand on the gear stick once!

'Did you ever see anything more beautiful in your life?'

To Liza's dismay, before she could reply to this remark, he was pulling in to park at the side of the road. How long did he intend drawing out her agony?

She turned a little stiffly towards the view he was pointing at. 'Yes, it's lovely,' she agreed. For there was no doubt that it was. Then she added, just to let him know that she had absorbed this first lesson and was ready to resume their journey just as soon as he chose, 'I've got to admit I've never seen scenery like it. It's so green, yet so amazingly wild and rugged.'

'It gets even wilder and greener if you go up into the hills. You should try that some time. You can easily borrow a pair of walking shoes.'

'Walking shoes?' Liza laughed. 'No, I can't see me doing that. I'm afraid I'm not really much into walking.'

'Well, if you don't fancy walking, we can go riding again some time.'

He smiled as he said it, his dark eyes brushing against her face. And, caught unawares by that reference to yesterday, to her dismay, Liza felt herself blushing furiously.

She kept her gaze averted. 'No, I don't think we'll bother, thanks. In fact, if I had to choose,' she added in a clipped tone, swallowing hard and struggling to compose herself, 'I think I'd very definitely prefer walking.'

Richard was still watching her. 'Don't worry,' he told her. 'Next time we go riding we'll have a horse each and I promise we'll definitely take it a bit slower.'

That simply served to increase her blushes. Had he guessed, Liza found herself wondering in agony, that yesterday's mad ride with him across the meadow had been the most thrilling experience of her life?

In case he had, she assured him firmly now, 'You'll never get me on a horse again. I may be required to start learning a bit about them, but I've no desire whatsoever to get up on their backs.'

'Don't you want to learn to ride?'

'Whatever for? Definitely not!'

'Pity.' He smiled at her. 'I was rather looking forward to teaching you.'

'Teaching me?'

As she looked back at him, something jolted inside Liza. The way he was looking at her and the slight inflection in his voice had made the suggestion sound oddly seductive. And she had responded in spite of herself. She had felt her blood leap. Just for an instant she had rather fancied the idea of being Richard's pupil.

She pushed the feeling from her and forced herself to answer coolly, 'I really don't think there's any need for that. The ability to ride is the last thing I'm ever likely to have any need for.'

'Not even to impress your friends?' He winked as he said it. 'Don't you think it would be worth it just for that?'

'No, I don't, as a matter of fact.' Liza pulled a face, trying hard not to smile in response. For he'd made the remark good-humouredly, without malice, simply teasing her. And, though she knew she shouldn't care, Liza felt oddly relieved that he hadn't misjudged her, after all.

And now he was saying, reaching for the doorhandle, 'Let's relax for five minutes. Let's go and take a closer look at the view.'

'Shouldn't we be getting back?' As he jumped down, Liza protested. She had no desire to prolong this uncomfortable twosome. She wanted to get back to where there were other people about.

She did her best to sound businesslike. 'Those phone calls you have to make... Didn't you say that they were urgent?'

'No, I didn't, as a matter of fact. And, don't worry, they can wait.' Richard smiled and held her eyes for a moment. 'But, all the same, I'm impressed that you're taking your job so seriously. Good girl.' He winked at her. 'Keep it up.'

Damn him! As he moved away, Liza glared after him. He knew she didn't like being alone with him like this. But at least now that he'd left the car it wasn't so bad. She could relax a little and breathe more easily.

She watched as he crossed on leisurely strides to the wooden fence that bounded the field beyond the road and leaned against it, his eyes fixed on the distant hills. He was probably just doing this because he knew she wanted to get back. Tormenting her seemed to be his favourite occupation.

She grimaced—well, what else could you expect from a Hawkes?—and decided it might be rather satisfying to needle him right back.

Besides, there was something supremely irritating about the way he was leaning against that fence, the broad shoulders taut beneath the plain grey shirt, one booted foot resting against the crossbar of the fence.

Opening her window, she poked her head out. 'You know,' she observed, 'you haven't actually told me yet what hours I'm supposed to work. I presume,' she added sarcastically, 'that I do get some time off?'

'Can't hear you.' As he spoke, he didn't even bother to turn round. 'You'll have to get out if you want to pursue a conversation.'

Liza felt her hackles rise. Wretched man! She knew perfectly well he'd heard every word!

Still, she repeated her query, this time a little louder.

'What hours precisely am I supposed to work?'

But she was wasting her breath. He didn't answer. Instead, he observed, as though to himself, 'You know, this is one of my favourite spots...' Then he pointed towards the hills. 'See that peak over there...? The rocky bit behind the trees...'

As he paused, Liza glared at him, her eyes picking holes in him, totally ignoring his outstretched arm. Damn and blast him! she was thinking. I could happily wring his neck!

'It's a great place for a picnic. You ought to go there some time.' He carried on, sublimely untouched by her fury. 'It's about an hour's walk,' he informed her, still in that detached tone, causing Liza's hands to clench into tight fists in her lap. 'I often go up there. It's called Blake's Rock.'

What?

Liza stiffened, her eyes swivelling round to stare at the spot where he was pointing. Then she was down out of the Range Rover like a shot. In a flash she was standing right beside him.

'Why is it called that?' she wanted to know.

Richard half-turned to look at her. 'That's a very interesting story. Maybe one day when we have more time I'll tell it to you,' he replied.

'Can't you tell me it now? I'd love to hear it!' This sounded like a perfect story for Aunt Julia!

'No, I'm afraid not.' His tone was implacable and Liza experienced a sudden *frisson* of worry that he had set her up, that he had somehow found out that her name was Blake and she was about to be torn apart for lying to him.

But, as he shook his head and smiled a slow smile, she realised she needn't worry. There was a much less devious explanation for why he wasn't going to tell her the story.

She had sounded too keen. It was as simple as that. For hadn't she always known he would make a point of thwarting her if he even suspected he knew what she was after? From now on she must be a little more careful.

Liza glanced away and shrugged. 'Oh, well, it doesn't matter. As you said, some other time, perhaps.' Then she turned to look at him again, her eyes carefully expressionless. 'Actually, I'm much more interested in having an answer to my earlier question. What hours am I supposed to work?'

'Ah, yes . . .' Richard turned round more fully to face her. 'I should have told you. You'll work whatever hours I need you and you'll have one and a half days off a week. At least, you will if I can spare you. If I can't spare you, I'll pay you extra.' He flicked her a smile. 'Are you quite happy with that?'

'Delirious.'

Quite frankly, it was of no importance. She'd only brought the subject up in the first place because he made her angry. She wouldn't be staying around long enough for such details to matter. Though, it struck her that, if she were, she might be less than happy. The details he'd outlined sounded a bit like slave labour.

She threw him an oblique look. 'Now I understand,' she told him, 'why your previous assistant went off and left you in the lurch.' So much for Penny's claim that his staff all adored him!

But Richard merely laughed. 'My previous assistant was devoted.' Then he smiled a wry smile. 'At least, she was until a short while ago. But then she met this Frenchman who was over here on holiday, fell hopelessly in love and last week ran off to France to get married.'

He raised one dark eyebrow and glanced across at her. 'I hope you're not planning to do anything similar.'

'Run off and get married? No, I shouldn't think so.'

'So, there's no boyfriend, then? At least, no one serious.'

'As a matter of fact there is.' Liza found herself blushing. Strangely, when he'd made that remark about running off to get married, she hadn't even thought of Elliott.

Though it wasn't strange, she told herself. It would be a bit premature if she had. She and Elliott hadn't quite got round to discussing marriage!

Still, she put Richard right. 'I do have a serious boyfriend.'

'Is he jealous?'

'Not particularly.'

'Good.'

'Why do you ask?'

This conversation was taking a peculiar turn, she was thinking. What was he about to come up with next?

But Richard was glancing at his watch and changing the subject. 'Hey, it's getting late. We'd better be getting back.' Then he was leading her on long strides back to the Range Rover.

But Liza's curiosity was getting the better of her. As they reached the car, she turned to look at him. 'Why did you ask if my boyfriend was jealous?'

He smiled. 'Because I wouldn't like to get you into trouble.'

'What kind of trouble?'

'Boyfriend trouble.' As she frowned, he elaborated, 'You see, the day after tomorrow—Friday, that is—I have a rather important lunch date lined up. One of the owners and his wife are coming to the castle. I need someone, shall we say, to make up the numbers... And, anyway, the wives prefer it when there's a hostess to chat to... So I thought you, my dear Miss Hardcastle, would fit the bill perfectly...'

In a gesture of mock gallantry, he pulled open the passenger door for her. 'On Friday you can do me the honour of posing as my girlfriend.'

'Do *what*? You must be joking! I'll do no such thing!'

'Of course you will. And you'll do it perfectly. You're ideal for the job.' He continued to stand there, quite clearly thoroughly enjoying her consternation. 'Besides, who knows? You might even enjoy it.'

'I doubt that very much.' Liza would have continued the argument, but she had become aware of the way he was standing over her as he held the car door open, waiting for her to climb inside. And the sudden awareness was giving her goosebumps all over. Why, he was virtually standing right on top of her!

Abandoning her argument, she scuttled inside, pulling the door shut quickly behind her.

'And now that we've got that settled, let's get back to the office.'

A moment later Richard was climbing into the driver's seat beside her, slamming his door shut and sticking the key in the ignition. Then they were heading off down the road towards the castle with a slightly dazed Liza staring unseeingly out through the windscreen.

How on earth did I get into this? she was wondering. And what the devil is this man going to get me into next?

CHAPTER FOUR

LIZA had rather hoped she might be gone before the lunch date with Richard's friends. Of all the tasks she'd suddenly been landed with this was the one she fancied least.

Getting the hang of the office records was one thing, after all. Even working with the horses she could manage to steel herself to. But having to pose as Richard's girlfriend? That was really a bit much!

Still, there was no point in making a fuss. It sounded harmless enough. And, besides, she knew that the more she protested, the more Richard would insist and the harder he would make things for her.

Direct opposition was not the way to handle Richard Hawkes. That was a fact she was rapidly latching on to. If she was to get round him, she must learn to employ subtler tactics.

This was one of the reasons she hadn't mentioned Blake's Rock again. If she appeared too interested, he would never tell her the story. And it was also why she had decided to be very careful about how she went about gaining access to the ballroom.

In the two days she'd been here she'd taken masses of photographs of various rooms inside the castle. For, in spite of his threat to stick to her like a limpet, Richard wasn't at her side quite twenty-four hours a day, and Liza had used to the full every moment of freedom!

She'd done most of her snapping late last night after she was supposed to be in bed.

Up in her rose-coloured bedroom she'd waited half an hour or so until it seemed likely that Richard wouldn't disturb her. They'd had dinner together earlier in the sumptuous dining-room, a turn up for the books that had rather surprised her. She'd half expected to be banished to the kitchen! And it had been a civil enough meal, though Richard had left before coffee.

'You'll have to forgive me,' he'd told her, as Mrs Donnelly cleared away the fruit plates. 'I'm going to have coffee upstairs in my study. I have some papers I want to look at before I turn in.'

Liza had watched him go, smiling as the housekeeper muttered, 'He works too hard. It can't be good for him. Sometimes he's shut up in that little study of his next to his bedroom until one or two o'clock in the morning.'

No rest for the wicked, Liza had thought to herself with satisfaction, grateful that he was finally out of her hair. And that was when she'd decided to seize the moment.

Dressed in her blue towelling robe, with her camera tucked under her arm, she'd sneaked out of her room just before midnight. By now, she'd been thinking, the coast would be clear. Richard would be well immersed in his papers.

First, she'd crept downstairs, snapping as she went, and had taken virtually half a roll of pictures of the now deserted dining room. The wonderful mahogany table with its graceful Sheraton dining chairs. The magnificent inlaid sideboard. The display of gleaming Sèvres porcelain. Aunt Julia was going to love all this!

Then she'd taken some shots of the hall before sneaking back upstairs again, rather pleased with her secret night's work.

But she was in for a shock, for at the top of the stairs she'd almost walked straight into Richard.

'Sleep-walking, were we?' His tone was cutting. Clearly, sleep-walking was the last thing he actually believed she'd been doing.

'I was just taking a walk. I couldn't sleep. I went down to the kitchen for something to drink.'

As Liza rattled off this lie, privately rather shocked at herself, she surreptitiously hid her camera behind her back. There was always a chance he hadn't spotted it.

'My, you're up late!' she added, trying to look innocent. 'Did you manage to finish those papers you had to look at?'

'Eventually. Thank heavens.'

He smiled as he answered and it occurred to Liza that perhaps he appreciated her show of interest. She faked a look of concern. 'It's not good to work so late. No one should still be at their desk at midnight.'

'It's a busy time of year and the work has to be done.' Richard leaned lightly against the banisters and gave a small shrug. 'But, I must confess, I'm certainly ready for bed now.'

'You must be. You must be exhausted.'

And he did look a little tired, Liza found herself thinking as she looked into his face. The stubbly shadow of beard darkened his chin and there was a faint suggestion of hollows around his eyes. Even the glossy dark hair that fell over his forehead seemed to flop a little tiredly.

Poor Richard, she thought gently, feeling a thrust of sudden warmth for him. For he seemed suddenly a little less invincible than usual. Not vulnerable, exactly. But there was just a little less edge to him.

She smiled at him, this time with genuine sympathy. 'I won't hold you up, then.' She made to move past him. 'I'll let you get off to bed.'

But she was going nowhere. As lithe as a panther, he had stepped in front of her. 'Haven't you forgotten something?' he demanded through his teeth.

Liza blinked at him in bewilderment and took a hurried step back. 'What on earth do you mean?' she stuttered.

'I mean I'm waiting for an explanation.'

He was standing right in front of her, blocking her path, and there was no sign now of his earlier tiredness. His eyes sparked at her, as bright and as sharp as needles.

'An explanation for what?'

'An explanation for this!' All at once, he was snatching her by the arm and exposing the camera she still had hidden behind her back. 'You haven't explained what you were doing with this!'

Liza was shell-shocked for a moment. The transformation had been so instant. But through her shock she also felt furious with herself. How could she have allowed herself to feel even a shred of warmth for this monstrous, perfectly despicable bully? Boy, was she crazy! Talk about gullible!

She tried to tug her arm away. 'It's only a camera! I wasn't doing any harm! You'd think it was a bomb or something!'

Richard did not find that funny. His grip around her arm grew tighter. Impatiently, he shook her. 'What were you doing with it? Why were you sneaking around my house after midnight, secretly taking pictures?' He shook her again. 'I presume that's what you were doing?'

It would be futile to lie. It was obvious what she'd been doing.

Liza glared at him, suddenly full of angry indignation. 'Yes, that is what I was doing. A perfectly innocent occupation. I don't know why you're getting so het-up about it!'

'I'm getting het-up because you had no business taking photographs.' Anger flew from his eyes like sparks from an anvil. 'Are you in the habit of taking pictures inside other people's houses without permission? Don't you think it would have been polite to ask first whether I minded?'

Liza felt her anger dribble away guiltily. He was right, of course, and in any other circumstances, naturally, she would have asked permission.

She pulled a face and told him honestly, 'I didn't ask because I knew you'd say no.'

Richard smiled a small smile. 'And why would I say no, if your intentions, as you seem to be insisting, were wholly innocent?'

'Because you always say no. You always go against me. And I had no reason to believe that this time would be any different.'

'Perhaps you should have tried me. You might have been surprised.'

'Does that mean you don't mind? That I can take more photographs?' Liza, frankly, didn't believe it for an instant. 'Because I'd really like to take some more, if it's OK.'

'Ask me some other time.' He subjected her to a long look, then as though he had suddenly grown tired of the conversation, abruptly he released her, though he continued to stand over her. 'But take no more pictures in future without asking my permission. Otherwise, I shall be forced to confiscate the camera.' His eyes bored into her. 'Do you understand?'

Liza glared at him. 'Yes, I understand,' she answered.

'Good.'

He submitted her to one last hard glance. Then he was turning on his heel and marching off down the corridor.

Liza had taken no more photographs inside the house since then, though her reasons for not doing so were not strictly honourable.

She had no desire for a repeat of last night's confrontation and she knew it would be pointless to ask Richard's permission, for there was no doubt in her mind that he would say no.

He would probably have said no anyway, even before that little bust-up, but he was absolutely certain to do so now. For he knew now that not only did she want to take some photographs, but that she wanted pretty badly to take them. No one went around secretly snapping at midnight unless they were keen!

But, all the same, Liza had decided she was prepared to defy him one more time—although only in order to get some pictures of the ballroom. So, this morning, she'd snatched a few minutes alone with the housekeeper and asked her the first thing she needed to know... Where exactly was the ballroom?

'It's on the first floor in the west wing,' Mrs Donnelly had told her, glancing up from the silver candelabra she was polishing. 'And a fine room it is, too. You'll never see finer. You must ask Mr Hawkes to show you round it some time.'

'Oh, I don't think I need trouble him. I can just go and take a look myself.'

Liza had already been rubbing her hands mentally at the prospect. I can photograph it tonight, when he thinks I'm asleep, she'd been calculating, and be on my way out of here first thing tomorrow morning!

But Mrs Donnelly had dashed that hope. 'I'm afraid you'll have to ask Mr Hawkes. You see, the ballroom's kept locked and only Mr Hawkes has the key.'

'You mean it's locked *all* the time?'

'I'm afraid so.' The housekeeper nodded. 'You see it's full of treasures. Priceless paintings and all sorts of things. But, don't worry, I'm sure Mr Hawkes will be delighted to show you round.'

Fat chance! Liza went to bed that night feeling distinctly dispirited. Richard might just agree to show her the ballroom, but never in a million years would he allow her to take photographs. And she needed photographs to take back to Aunt Julia!

She stared into the darkness. Earlier she'd phoned Elliott and told him she wouldn't be able to come back just yet.

'I need a couple of more days, at least,' she'd sighed. Then she'd groaned. 'Lord, I'm going to end up having to stay a whole week unless some kind of miracle comes along!'

'Why not just give up now and come back to London?' Elliott had tried to persuade her.

But she'd insisted, 'No, I can't just give up. I've got to find a way of cracking this.'

And now as she lay beneath the bedclothes, staring into the darkness, she was even more determined than ever. Richard Hawkes wouldn't beat her. She'd get what she wanted, even if she had to fight him every inch of the way!

Then she stopped herself. That was wrong. Hadn't she already decided that direct confrontation with Richard wouldn't work? What she ought to be thinking of doing was employing a bit of subtlety.

And suddenly it came to her. And it was so perfect and so obvious. Richard was a man, with all a man's susceptibilities, and she was a woman, with all a woman's special skills. Perhaps she could flatter him into co-operation. Butter him up a little. Play to his ego.

Soften him up, that was what she'd do. Then, when she'd got what she wanted, she'd blow him a big raspberry and scarper!

Liza smiled to herself and stretched beneath the sheets. She had the feeling she was going to rather enjoy this new approach!

'I'm afraid our guests are going to be a little late. While we're waiting, why don't you join me for a drink out on the terrace?'

Richard was waiting in the drawing-room when Liza appeared to join him, at twelve-thirty precisely, as arranged.

She paused in the doorway as he stood up to greet her. 'OK,' she smiled. 'That sounds nice.' And there wasn't even a trace of irony in her voice.

After much thought, Liza had decided to dress simply for their lunch date—in a slim white skirt and a shell-pink top. She had a rather special jade-green dress that she'd mulled over for a while, but in the end she'd decided against it. She didn't want to look as though she was laying it on too thick. Richard wasn't a fool. He might smell a rat.

For she'd been behaving like a perfect angel all morning, smiling at him and agreeing with him and never once crossing swords with him, exactly as she'd promised herself in bed last night.

When he'd told her, 'Make this phone call,' or, 'Find these figures for me,' she'd gone ahead and done it as though there was nothing she'd rather be doing. She'd even managed to keep her smile in place at the stables when he'd told her to give Ken, one of the stable lads, a hand at rubbing down one of the horses. Never did any man have a more willing and good-natured little helpmate!

It was hard to tell yet if it was working, but it certainly wasn't doing any damage. He hadn't exactly rolled over and surrendered at this sudden display of charm, but then that was the last thing Liza had expected. All she'd hoped for at this stage was that he might have grown a little mellow, a little less spiky around edges. And maybe, just maybe, that was precisely what was happening.

At any rate, he was being the perfect gentleman as he crossed now to the bar and indicated the array of bottles. 'What can I get you?' he was asking.

For once he had changed out of his habitual jeans or jodhpurs and was wearing a rather snappy pair of cream cotton trousers, with a perfectly toning cream and lemon striped shirt, tan loafers and a matching brass-buckled tan belt.

He looks good dressed like that, Liza found herself thinking. But then he would look good however he dressed. He had the perfect build, tall and broad-shouldered, and the graceful, upright carriage of a rider that enabled him to carry off clothes with panache. He might be an abomination in all other respects, but it was hard not to admire the way he looked.

Not admire, just observe, Liza corrected herself hastily. She took a step into the room. 'I'd like a tonic water,' she said.

'One tonic water coming up.' As he bent over the bottles, his hair flopped glossily over his forehead. He shot her a glance. 'You're looking rather lovely. I was beginning to wonder if you had legs.'

To her annoyance, Liza blushed, though he probably hadn't noticed. He had turned to drop ice into a couple of glasses.

'Is this really the first time I've worn a skirt?'

Liza shrugged an innocent shrug as she answered, but actually she wasn't being totally truthful. For it *had* struck her earlier, upstairs in her room, while she was examining her freshly shaved legs in the mirror and observing that, thank heavens, they still had a nice tan, that this was the first time since she'd come to the castle that she hadn't worn trousers.

She smiled now. 'It makes a nice change to wear a skirt.'

Richard was walking towards her, holding out her glass to her. 'I appreciate the gesture. Personally, I'm a legs man.'

Liza almost glared at him then, but she stopped herself in time. Glaring was out. She was supposed to be buttering him up. So she forced herself to smile sweetly instead.

'Don't mention it,' she purred. 'We aim to please.'

'Follow me.'

He was leading her across the drawing-room to the terrace that overlooked the rose garden, bathed now in gentle summer sunshine. There were some chairs in the shade and a little wooden table. Richard seated himself and, with a wave of his hand, invited Liza to do the same.

In the light of that last comment of his, Liza was very careful about the way she lowered herself into her seat. Her, 'We aim to please,' had very definitely been tongue in cheek. Thank heavens she wasn't wearing one of her shorter skirts!

Richard took a mouthful of his drink and glanced at her over the top of it. 'So, how did you enjoy your walk this morning?'

'Very much, as a matter of fact.' Liza smiled as she answered. And it was a genuine smile. She had no need to fake. For she had greatly enjoyed her tramp across the moor with Penny this morning.

It was Richard who had suggested that she go.

'Penny's got an errand to do over at one of the farms a couple of miles away. Why don't you go with her? I won't be needing you for the next hour or so.'

Liza had jumped at the chance, even though country walks weren't exactly a passion of hers. It was a rare chance to spend some time without Richard breathing down her neck, though she couldn't help wondering if Penny had been asked to keep an eye on her in his place!

But, even if that were so, it hadn't spoiled her enjoyment. 'It was beautiful,' she told Richard now. 'And I'm sure the exercise did me good. I just wished I'd taken my camera with me.'

As soon as she said that, Liza wished she hadn't. Her camera, after all, was a bit of a sore point between them.

But Richard merely smiled. 'You've got plenty of time to take photographs.' He continued to hold her eyes for a moment. 'If you're good, one day I'll take you to see some of our famous beauty spots.'

'That would be nice.'

Liza fluttered him a look. It was all part of her act—her buttering-up act—but all the same there'd been a warmth in his voice and in his eyes that, quite illogically, she'd felt herself responding to. Just for a moment she'd felt perhaps it really would be nice to visit some of the local beauty spots with him, and that fluttering look had come just a little too easily. I must be going mad, she thought.

But now he proceeded to change the subject.

He sat back in his seat and put to her in a light tone, 'So, how does your boyfriend feel about your growing love of the English countryside?'

'My boyfriend?'

Liza's eyebrows lifted as she threw him an oblique look. Last night, when she'd asked his permission to phone London, she hadn't told him who she was calling. That had just been a lucky guess on his part.

She shrugged now and added, 'We didn't discuss the English countryside. It's not a subject that would interest Elliott.'

'Another townie, I see?' There was a note of teasing in Richard's voice.

Liza pulled a face and nodded. 'Yes, very definitely, another townie. And an even more hardened case than me. Elliott was born and bred in New York City.'

'A New Yorker, eh? So, what's he doing in London?'

'He's working for an American bank in the City. Only temporarily. He's been over for a year. He goes back to the States with me in September.'

'Nice. A banker.' Richard smiled. 'That's always handy.'

Liza smiled back, but she was wishing they could change the subject. This discussion about her boyfriend was rather cramping her style. How could you flutter your eyelashes at a man who insists on discussing your boyfriend?

But, before she could divert him, Richard was asking, 'So, if it's serious, as you said it was, how come you're not planning to run off and get married?'

'Maybe we will one day.' Liza shrugged and added, 'Neither of us is in any hurry at the moment.'

'So, he's a bit cautious, is he, your Elliott? I suppose that comes from being a banker. As a breed they're not much given to rushing into things.'

'Neither are you, it seems.' Liza shot the remark at him. She didn't care for the way he seemed to be poking fun at Elliott. 'After all, you don't appear to have rushed into anything either.'

'You mean marriage?' Richard seemed surprised for a moment by her attack. Then he reached for his glass and smiled across at her. 'My trouble is I'm too fond of the chase.'

Liza looked at him. Yes, that made sense, she was thinking. She had vaguely wondered why he wasn't married and why there didn't appear to be any steady girlfriend around. But now she understood. He was a bit of a Don Juan. He preferred to enjoy his women without ties, and probably never stuck around for long with any of them.

To use his own words, he enjoyed the chase. Once he'd made his conquest, he'd instantly lose interest and simply go on to the next one.

She derived an oddly disappointing sense of satisfaction from knowing that.

It was at that moment that Mrs Donnelly appeared in the drawing-room doorway.

'Mr Hawkes, sir,' she informed Richard, 'your guests have arrived.'

Richard rose instantly to his feet with a broad smile on his face, as a bearded, bespectacled man and a beautiful dark-haired woman appeared in the doorway beside the housekeeper.

'Welcome,' he told them, stepping towards them. 'Come and sit down. I'm glad you finally made it.'

Then he turned to Liza, touching her arm lightly as he did so. 'Allow me to introduce you. This is my good friend Liza Hardcastle. Emmeline and Ivan Kinsky.'

As she shook hands with his guests, who seemed a delightful couple, Liza felt that customary jolt inside her to hear herself introduced as Liza Hardcastle. Sometimes she wished she'd never told that lie about her name. It had gone so far now, he'd be furious if he ever found out.

But there was another reason, too, for the jolt inside her, for suddenly she was feeling a little uneasy in her role.

How well did the Kinskys know Richard? she was wondering. Were they aware of his love of the chase? And, if they knew he was a Don Juan, what were they thinking of her? Were they smiling to themselves secretly and assuming she was just another of his conquests? Somehow, she didn't like that idea at all.

But as she exchanged pleasantries with them and they all seated themselves out on the terrace, she told herself briskly not to be so stupid. It didn't matter what they thought. She wasn't one of his conquests. She wasn't even the 'good friend' he'd claimed her to be. And all this was simply a silly but harmless charade that she must sensibly use to her advantage—another step in the process of buttering Richard up!

Emmeline and Ivan were quite as delightful as they'd first seemed. After drinks out on the terrace, they all moved into the dining-room where Mrs

Donnelly proceeded to serve a positive banquet of a lunch, and Liza found to her surprise that she was rather enjoying herself.

The talk around the table touched on all sorts of subjects, though even when it turned to horses Liza was able to join in quite happily. After all, she was no longer a complete novice in that area! And she discovered she rather enjoyed listening to Richard's amusing anecdotes.

She regarded him beneath her lashes with grudging approval. One thing you had to say for him, he was an entertaining host.

'Are you a country girl, Liza?' As they all tucked into a delicious roast beef, Emmeline turned to glance at Liza. 'You look as though you might be. With that wonderful skin and that gorgeous auburn hair of yours you look like a girl who'd be very much at home in the great outdoors.'

Liza was unexpectedly pleased by the compliment. 'Actually, I'm a townie,' she smiled. 'Though I'm learning to quite enjoy the countryside.'

She'd said it out of politeness, but there was truth in it, she realised. The countryside, surprisingly, did have its attractions!

'I'm doing my best to win her round.' Richard winked across at her, catching her unawares and causing her to blush like an idiot. 'If I have my way, before the summer's out she'll have stopped even thinking of herself as a townie.'

Liza met his gaze and smiled lightly back at him, trying to ignore the strange reaction inside her. For a flickering moment she'd found herself regretting that before the summer was out she'd be long gone from here. Back home on the other side of the Atlantic. Far from Abbotsdale Castle, the Yorkshire countryside and Richard.

I'm mad, she told herself. I must have drunk too much wine! The sooner I'm gone, the happier I'll be!

As the meal progressed, the conversation moved to other things. The Kinskys talked a bit about their home in Switzerland.

'You must visit us again soon,' Ivan told Richard, slanting a quick glance across at Liza as he did so, politely including her in the invitation.

Liza nodded a brief acknowledgement but reflected with a wry smile that Ivan knew as well as she did that she would never take up the invitation. Even if her current supposed romance with Richard were real he would have moved on to pastures new long before he went to Switzerland.

Countering that earlier tipsy feeling of regret, she told herself now that all she felt was sympathy for whoever Richard's companion to Switzerland would be. Just another soon-to-be-discarded conquest.

It was as they were being served coffee that Liza unexpectedly found herself with a wonderful opportunity to cash in on the situation.

The talk had moved from Switzerland to Abbotsdale and Yorkshire, with the two guests singing the praises of the wonderful local countryside.

'It's so beautiful,' Emmeline enthused. 'So green, yet so rugged.'

A switch flicked in Liza's brain. She hesitated for only an instant, then, keeping her gaze carefully averted from Richard, she leaned across the table towards Emmeline. 'Have you ever visited Blake's Rock?' she asked her. 'That's one of the loveliest spots around here.'

'No, I haven't. But I've heard of it.' Emmeline glanced at her husband. 'We must try and go there some time.'

'You must. It's a wonderful spot for a picnic. And Richard tells me...' At last, Liza turned to glance at Richard. Now she was coming to the point of this little diversion! 'Richard tells me there's a fascinating story attached to it.'

'Oh, Richard, do tell us!' Emmeline turned to him and wheedled. 'I do love hearing your Abbotsdale stories.'

So, Richard had no choice. He proceeded to tell the story, though not before slanting an amused glance at Liza. Congratulations! That was pretty neat, his smile seemed to be telling her.

He sat back in his chair. 'Well, I don't know how true it is, but the story goes that about a hundred years ago there was this chap called Blake who got lost up in the hills during a winter snowstorm. He was missing for days. Everyone thought he was dead. But just when the whole village had given up hope, his sheepdog found him up on the rock and guided him down...'

He paused to glance at Liza's still, rapt face. 'And, ever since then, it's been called Blake's Rock.'

'What a lovely story.' Aunt Julia would love it! Liza was thinking. She held his eyes. 'Do you know any more stories like that?'

'Dozens.'

'Really?'

'Maybe one day I'll tell you them.'

'Oh, you must get him to.' Emmeline was interrupting. 'He knows some of the most wonderful
stories I've ever heard.'

It was after four o'clock by the time the Kinskys
left to drive back to the friends they were staying
with near Bridlington—but with a promise to return
for dinner the following Monday. Richard and Liza
waved them off as they drove down the driveway
and disappeared at last out of view between the
trees.

Then Richard turned to Liza. 'I've got to go into
Abbotsdale. There's some rather urgent business I
have to see to.' He glanced at his watch. 'Would
you mind doing an hour or so at the office? Penny's
got a couple of little jobs lined up for you.'

'No, I don't mind.' Good heavens, Liza was
thinking, is he actually going to let me out of his
sight twice in one day? And had she misheard or,
instead of issuing his usual orders, had he actually
asked if she minded working for a couple of hours?
What was coming over the man?

He proceeded to surprise her further. Turning to
face her more fully, he told her, 'You did a good
job this lunchtime. I could tell Emmeline and Ivan
were quite bowled over by you.'

'Really?' She blushed. 'Well, it was no effort on
my part . I thought they were really lovely people.'

'It'll be rather nice to repeat the experience on
Monday when they come to dinner.' He reached
out unexpectedly and very softly touched her cheek.
'I hope I can count on your support again?'

'Of course.'

Liza's flesh was burning where he was touching
her. But she did not move away. She forced herself

to smile at him. He really is softening up, she was thinking. My tactics have started working already. For there was a warm look in his eyes as he continued to look down at her. She could feel it wrap itself around her, soft and seductive.

'So, you'd like to hear some stories?' His fingers were cupping her chin now. 'Well, maybe, since you did so well this afternoon, as a kind of reward, we might be able to arrange that.' His thumb brushed her lips ever so lightly. 'I would say you deserve a small reward.'

The sensation that shot through her as his thumb brushed her mouth would normally have caused Liza to step away. For it had felt like a searing hot bolt of electricity jolting its way deliciously down every one of her vertebrae and nailing her firmly to the floor.

But she made no effort to move away. She forced herself to endure it. After all, she told herself, she couldn't afford to reject him. He seemed to be softening up so nicely.

She said, a little hoarsely. 'Thank you. That would be nice.' Then, clearing her throat, she added quickly, 'I'd also be grateful if you'd let me take more pictures... And I'd quite like it if you'd show me round the ballroom.'

'The ballroom?'

'Yes. Mrs Donnelly was telling me all about it.'

She held her breath. Was she going too quickly? Should she perhaps not have mentioned the ballroom just yet? And there was another thing, too, that was worrying her slightly. She was beginning to feel just a little bit hypnotised by the power of the dark, grey- and amber-flecked eyes.

As though she might not be able to move away,
even if she wished to.

And Richard's voice seemed to be coming from
very far away as he told her, 'OK. We'll see. But
not tonight, I'm afraid. I suspect I'm going to be
tied up till pretty late.' He brushed her mouth lightly
with the flat of his thumb again. 'Possibly, we can
do it tomorrow.'

'Tomorrow. Good.'

Her mouth was as dry as cinders. The way he
was looking at her and the way his thumb was
brushing against her lips was creating an uproar of
emotions inside her. Just looking back at him was
becoming increasingly difficult.

And then he took her by surprise. Suddenly he
leaned towards her and touched his lips very softly
to hers.

'I said possibly, remember? No promises,' he reminded her.

Then with a wink he turned and strode off across
the castle courtyard.

Liza was totally poleaxed for at least fifteen
minutes.

She walked back to the office feeling distinctly
dizzy. How had that happened? That hadn't been
meant to happen! There she'd been, thinking he
was softening up nicely... and now it rather looked
as though *she* was the one who'd gone soft! Just
like that, she'd let him kiss her!

It hadn't been much of a kiss, she tried to tell
herself. No more than the briefest touch of his lips.
But it should never have happened. And, rather

more to the point, she most definitely shouldn't have enjoyed it!

For she had. It had electrified her, from her scalp to her toenails. She had never known a kiss half so exciting in her life!

Just thinking that made her angry—both with Richard and with herself. He was a Don Juan, all right. An expert seducer. How cleverly he'd lured her into that kiss and how easily tricked and naïve she'd been. Well, she'd be making darned sure it didn't happen again!

To Liza's relief, Richard didn't appear for dinner.

She had dinner in the dining-room alone. Then before bed she tried to phone Elliott—to pass on the good news that it looked as though she'd soon be on her way back to London. As Richard had pointed out, he hadn't *promised* to show her the ballroom, but all the same he'd come within a whisker. If she played her cards right—though with a degree of caution!—she was pretty sure she could persuade him.

But there was no reply at Elliott's flat and his answering machine wasn't working, so Liza went to bed without being able to speak to him. Never mind, she told herself, she would call him again tomorrow, once she was more certain how things stood.

And in the meantime she concentrated on congratulating herself on her achievement. Her spell of purgatory was nearly over. No more having to work when she was supposed to be on holiday! No more having to run around after Richard! Knowing that was a huge relief.

But deep inside her there was another, far greater sense of relief, though one she didn't like to dwell on. For in her heart she knew it and it shamed her. It would be far too dangerous to stay on.

Next day Liza didn't see Richard till nearly lunchtime.

When she arrived at the office at nine o'clock sharp, Penny—who worked a half-day on Saturdays—told her, 'He's gone to a couple of appointments in the village. But don't worry,' she laughed, 'he's left a pile of work for you!'

Liza set about her pile of work almost enthusiastically. What was there to complain about? This was her last day here. And, anyway, though she would never have admitted it to Richard, she actually quite enjoyed the work!

Just before lunch she borrowed a bike and went round to the stables with some documents that Jim, the stable manager, had asked for. And she was feeling so keyed up at the thought of her imminent departure that she almost ran right into a man in a navy blazer who suddenly dashed across the path in front of her.

'Sorry!' she called out. But he didn't stick around for her apology. With a flash of brass buttons he'd disappeared up a side lane.

Never mind, Liza told herself. He's obviously OK. And then she thought no more about it.

She was at the stables, speaking to Joe, one of the stable lads, when the dark green Range Rover suddenly drew up and Richard leaned out of the window.

And just for a moment Liza felt her heart stutter, remembering that kiss, as she looked into his face. Just for a moment the ground seemed to shift a little.

But Richard's eyes were on Joe. 'Hi, Joe,' he called. Then he cast only the briefest of glances at Liza. 'Whenever you're ready,' he told her, 'I'll take you back to the castle.'

'Did you have a good morning?' A couple of minutes later, having pulled herself together and now with a bright smile on her face, Liza was climbing in beside him. 'I must say, I've had a pretty productive one.'

'Good.' He did not look at her and his tone was oddly clipped. A moment later, with a squeal of tyres, they were heading for the castle.

Liza chatted on a bit about what she'd been up to, but her overtures were met with stony silence. And there was something about the closed, harsh set of his profile that was beginning to worry her a little.

It was very clear that something had put him in a bad mood. She just hoped it wasn't going to affect their proposed visit to the ballroom.

They reached the courtyard behind the castle at last and Richard pulled on the handbrake. 'OK. We're here. Get out,' he told her in a rough tone.

Liza did as she was told. Good heavens, it *is* bad, she was thinking. Then, as he too climbed out and slammed the door shut behind him, a little tentatively she asked him, 'Is anything the matter?'

He did not answer her immediately. Then, for the first time, he looked at her.

'I was passing by your old boarding-house this morning,' he told her in a tone that was so cold it made her scalp prickle. 'So, I decided to drop in and see if there was any mail for you.' He paused and reached into his back jeans pocket and drew out a folded airmail letter. Unfolding it, he held it out to her. 'The landlady gave me this.'

Liza looked down at it, feeling the coldness in her scalp slowly spread right down to her toes. For on the front of the letter, in Aunt Julia's all-too-legible hand, was written the name 'Miss Liza Blake'.

She swallowed and glanced up into Richard's eyes, suddenly not knowing what to say.

But she wouldn't have had time to say anything anyway. For, eyes brimming with fury, Richard was snatching her by the arm and frog marching her unceremoniously across the courtyard.

'I want an explanation,' he growled. 'And it had better be good!'

CHAPTER FIVE

LIZA'S feet barely touched the ground as she was propelled across the courtyard. Then she was being whisked across the hallway and into the drawing-room and tossed almost bodily into a sofa by the window.

Richard stood over her, fulminating anger. 'Right,' he demanded, 'I want to know what's going on!' He tossed the incriminating letter at her and folded his arms across his chest.

Half buried among the cushions, Liza glared at him, trying to control the knocking of her heart against her ribs. She felt alarmed and shaken. He looked as though he might devour her. But she also felt outraged at being treated like this.

'There's really no need to start throwing your weight about! I'm not some kind of criminal, you know!' Her cheeks were flushed with fury as she pulled herself up against the cushions and stuffed Aunt Julia's letter into her pocket. 'Who the hell do you think you are, anyway?'

'Who am *I*? Who *I* am is not in question! What we're here to discuss is, who are *you*?' Richard glared back at her, dark eyes sparking like fire-crackers. 'That's what there seems to be a little confusion about.'

'Look, I can explain that.'

'Yes, I think you'd better—before I get on the phone and ask the police to come round.'

'The police? What are you talking about? What have the police to do with anything?'

As she looked at him, Liza felt a sharp dart of anxiety. Surely he had to be joking? He couldn't possibly be serious. Yet he didn't look, even remotely, as though he was joking.

'Don't look so innocent.' His eyes narrowed as he growled at her. 'You see, I know exactly who you are.'

'I'm Liza Blake.'

'Not Liza Hardcastle?' His tone twisted with angry accusation as he looked at her.

'No, that wasn't true. I admit I lied to you. But it was an innocent lie. I'm not a criminal.' She eyed him with a mixture of curiosity and apprehension. 'What did you mean when you said you knew who I was?'

By way of a response Richard simply glared at her. 'No, you first,' he commanded. 'You tell me who you are and why you lied to me if you're so innocent.'

He took a couple of steps back and, without detaching his eyes from hers, seated himself on the arm of a nearby armchair. As he leaned towards her, he had the look of a coiled spring, ready to pounce at the slightest provocation.

Liza had no intention of provoking him. All she wanted was to finally tell him the truth. But, before she began, she took a moment to compose herself, straightening her shoulders and crossing her legs at the ankles, as she leaned back lightly against the cushions.

'I lied to you,' she told him, 'because you put me on the defensive. That first day we met you were so obnoxious.' She regarded him levelly. 'It wasn't planned or deliberate. It was just something I did on the spur of the moment. I just felt the less I told you about myself, the better.'

'A likely story!' Richard laughed a scoffing laugh. 'Do you seriously expect me to swallow a load of nonsense like that? No one hides their true identity unless they have a very good reason.' He leaned towards her, dark eyes menacing. 'I'm afraid you'll have to do better than that.'

'I can't do better than that. I'm telling you the truth.' Liza frowned at him as she remembered the threat he'd made a moment ago. 'Why did you talk about bringing in the police? Surely it's not a criminal offence to lie about one's name in England?'

'I suspect it may be when that lie is intended to disguise criminal intentions.' Richard's expression was as hard and cold as diamonds. 'Perhaps we should give the local police a ring and find out?'

As he said it, he glanced at the phone on the nearby table. 'That might save both of us a great deal of time and trouble.'

'Then go ahead and phone them.' Maybe he should, Liza was thinking. Right from day one he seemed to have been peculiarly suspicious of her. Maybe it was time they finally got everything out in the open. 'I don't care if you bring in the entire Yorkshire police department,' she added.

'Well, that's fine, for it may well come to that.' Richard fixed her with a rapier look that, in spite of Liza's clear conscience, caused her heart to flutter a little. 'But, before we do that, I'd like to show you something.'

He stood up and crossed the room to a walnut bureau that stood against the wall in the far corner of the room, pulled open one of the drawers and drew out some papers. Then, grim-faced, he came to stand before her once again.

He held up the papers. 'Do you know what these are?'

'How can I know what they are? I can't even see them properly.'

'I thought you might recognise them. After all, they are quite distinctive.'

And they were. They looked like letters and each of them was written on a sheet of white paper with a solid black border.

Liza met Richard's gaze, 'They look like letters of condolence, but I'm afraid I've never set eyes on them before.'

'You didn't write them, then?'

'Write them? No, of course I didn't.'

'But you know who did.'

'I know no such thing.'

'I think you do. Let me refresh your memory.' Richard selected a letter at random and handed it to her.

Liza read the letter quickly, scarcely believing what she was reading. She had to sit back in her seat for a moment to take it in.

When she glanced up at Richard again, her cheeks were noticeably paler. 'This is monstrous,' she exclaimed. 'This letter is full of threats. How can you believe I could have written such a thing?'

Richard continued to stand over her and his expression had not softened. 'Why don't you tell me why I shouldn't believe it?' he challenged.

'Because it's outrageous, that's why!' Liza felt a shiver go through her as she glanced down with distaste at the letter in her hand. Never in her life had she read anything more horrible. She was not surprised that the only signature it bore was the anonymous but appropriate 'An Enemy'.

'Whoever wrote this letter is just plain evil,' she put to Richard. 'He's threatening to plant bombs in the castle, to poison your horses, to do all sorts of dreadful things...'

'He?'

'Well, of course it could be a she. But, even if it is, I can assure you it's not me.' There was an edge of undisguised outrage in Liza's voice. 'Surely you don't seriously believe it could be?'

'Why not?'

'Because it's ridiculous. It's ludicrous. And it's insulting.' She added that last protest with special feeling. For she did feel insulted, deeply insulted, that he could believe her to be mixed up in anything so foul. 'Besides,' she added, 'what possible motive could I have?'

'How do I know? Maybe you're some crank. Maybe you're mixed up in some crusade against horse-racing or something.' He snatched the letter from her hand and tossed it with the others on to the nearby chair. 'The world is full of such people who feel they have the right to take the law into their own hands.'

'Well, I'm not one of them!'

He really was serious. He really did believe she might be responsible. All at once, as she looked at him, Liza felt more than just insulted. She felt foolishly hurt and disappointed. They'd never exactly seen eye to eye, but surely he ought to know her better than that?

But it would appear he didn't. 'The evidence suggests otherwise.' Richard's tone was harsh as he continued, 'After all, you've been behaving like a criminal right from the very first moment we met.'

'You mean when you caught me up the tree?'

'Yes, trespassing on my land, secretly observing the castle.' His eyes narrowed. 'I ought to have turned you over to the police then. I thought about it and I should have just gone ahead and done it.'

Liza blinked at him. 'Surely you're not trying to tell me,' she protested, 'that you've been thinking, right from when you found me up that tree, that I had something to do with these awful letters?'

'It was the first thought that crossed my mind.' Richard's tone was steely. 'Your arrival coincided with the arrival of the last letter. And it so happens that the only reason I was riding through the woods was because I had a feeling there was someone out there up to no good. And, guess what?' He smiled without humour. 'I found you.'

Liza glared at him mutinously. The story was getting worse by the minute. 'So, why did you not just hand me over to the police? Since you were so sure, that would have been the logical thing to do.'

'I very nearly did, as I've already told you. But then I began to wonder if I might be mistaken. Maybe, after all, you were just an innocent, if trespassing, tourist. So instead of reporting you I decided I'd just keep an eye on you until I'd made up my mind about you.'

'So that was why you got me to come and work for you and why you've barely let me out of your

sight for ten minutes since!' Suddenly, belatedly, it
was all making sense to her. After all, there'd been
a purpose behind his watchful scrutiny. 'You've
been shadowing me like some one-man FBI in case
I tried to plant a bomb or something under your
bed!'

As she said it, she laughed. It was so ridiculous
it was funny. Then she sobered a little. 'Is that what
you thought the other night when you bumped into
me on the stairs?'

'That you were about to plant a bomb underneath my bed?' For the first time in this confrontation, Richard smiled. His expression lightened as
he looked at her, and for a moment he let his dark
eyes travel lazily over her. 'Perhaps, if I'd thought
you were on your way to my bedroom, I wouldn't
have been so keen to apprehend you.'

Liza felt herself blush. She should never have
brought beds into this. Especially not his bed. What
had possessed her?

She glanced down into her lap. 'Well, I wasn't,'
she assured him awkwardly. Then she glanced up
again, quickly recovering her poise, and told him,
'Though, if I had been, I can assure you, to plant
a bomb would have been the only reason.'

He was still smiling amusedly. 'What a pity,' he
said.

Lecherous beast. Liza scowled at him disapprov-
ingly, but all the same she had felt her skin prickle.
Just for a moment then her poor stomach had
twisted. Once again, like a bolt of lightning, she'd
felt his mouth brush her lips.

As she struggled to push the feeling from her,
Richard was continuing, stepping back a little and

thrusting his hands into his jeans pockets, 'I confess I did wonder at first what you were up to that night. But in the end I decided it was probably nothing criminal.

'In fact, overall, I'd more or less come to the conclusion that you weren't the author of these letters, after all. As you must have noticed, I left you on your own all this morning, as well as part of yesterday afternoon.'

Then he paused, his eyes narrowing and hardening as he added, 'But then, when I went to your old boarding house this morning and discovered you've been lying to me about who you really are, I'm afraid I changed my mind right back again!'

'But you're wrong!' Liza leapt to her feet to defend herself. 'I can see it looks suspicious, but you're way off track, I promise you! Just let me explain things and then you'll understand what's going on . . .'

'So, there *is* something going on?'

'In a way. Yes, I suppose so.'

'And you're not just some innocent, if overzealous tourist, like you originally claimed to be?'

'Not exactly, no. Though——'

She broke off awkwardly. I oughtn't to have stood up, she was thinking belatedly. The move had dramatically reduced the distance between them, and now he seemed to be standing right on top of her. She winced as he thundered, 'Then who the hell are you?'

Liza looked up into the dark eyes with their grey and amber flecks that were currently fixed on her in a kind of visual stranglehold and told him as calmly as she could, taking a sideways step away

from him, 'Why don't you calm down and give me
a chance to tell my story? Then you'll see how
wrong you've been about me.'

Richard remained standing where he was, feet
planted apart, and folded his arms across his broad
chest. 'OK,' he pronounced. 'Go ahead. I'm
listening.'

Liza launched straight in and told him everything. About Great-aunt Julia and her ancient con-
nections with the castle, and about the promise Liza
had made her to visit Abbotsdale and come back
with lots of photographs of the castle and its
ballroom.

'So, you see,' she concluded finally, pausing for
breath at last, 'it's all perfectly innocent, as I told
you, and I've got nothing to do with these horrible
letters.'

She dared to smile. Surely, he would be con-
vinced now, she was thinking.

But the expression on Richard's face, alas, suggested differently.

He had listened to her in silence, but now, stony-
eyed, he put to her, 'So, why if it's all so innocent
did you not just tell me all this at the very beginning? And why did you tell me your name was
Hardcastle?'

Liza had known he'd bring that up again and
she'd rather been dreading it. It was the hardest
part of the whole story to explain.

She glanced down at the floor, gathering her
thoughts for a moment. Then she raised her eyes
to his again and told him almost apologetically,
'The truth is I don't really know why I did it. It
was an instinctive reaction. It wasn't something I'd

planned.' Then she narrowed her eyes accusingly. 'You made me do it.'

'*I* made you do it?' Richard laughed out loud, dismissively. 'That's a good one. Kindly explain.'

'Well, you came on to me so aggressively. You on your big horse! How do you think I felt?' Her green eyes sparked at him. 'You were deliberately trying to scare me, to put me on the defensive. And I just suddenly had this feeling that I shouldn't tell you who I was. After all, you didn't tell me who you were!'

'I didn't lie to you, either.'

'No. You were just evasive. Evasive and bullying and overbearing.' She tossed her head at him. 'A typical Hawkes, if I may say so!'

Richard laughed again, but this time with amusement. 'And what would you know about a typical Hawkes?'

'I know plenty. My Aunt Julia's told me lots of stories. We're Blakes, remember? And the Hawkes have always hated the Blakes. No one knows what a typical Hawkes is better than a Blake!'

'Oh, really? Is that so?' He was continuing to smile at her. 'So, tell me, what exactly is a typical Hawkes?' As he spoke, he had taken a step towards her. 'Go on. Don't be shy. I'd love to know.'

Liza looked up into his face, aware that something had altered dramatically. A moment ago the air had been black with anger, but now, although it continued to shimmer strangely, all the blackness and the anger had drained away. Now, in place of anger, there was a sense of danger and excitement.

She swallowed. 'I don't know. I was talking nonsense, I suppose.'

All at once, she seemed to be burning, from her scalp down to her toes.

Then suddenly Richard smiled. 'I didn't realise your eyes were so green.' He was gazing closely into her face, though he still hadn't touched her. 'They really are an amazingly vivid colour.'

'They change with the light and depending on what I happen to be wearing.'

Liza was aware that her heart was suddenly beating too quickly and that she really ought not to be standing like this with him. But she did not move, except to tilt her head a bit, so that she could see him better.

'I suppose they're greener now because I'm wearing a green shirt,' she explained.

'They're like emeralds.' Richard smiled. 'I've never seen such lovely eyes.'

'Really?'

Liza smiled back foolishly. She really ought to move. This whole situation was getting too dangerous and any minute now she was going to regret it.

'Are they typical Blake eyes?' His gaze continued to pour over her. 'If they are, I must say I'm rather partial.'

'I don't know if they're typical, but my Great-aunt Julia's are the same.'

Still, she did not move. She continued to gaze back at him recklessly, feeling as though her feet had been glued to the carpet.

'And that nose of yours... Is it a typical Blake nose?' Richard reached up then to take her chin with his fingers and guide her head round gently to show him her profile. 'Yes, I think I rather like this Blake face.'

Liza felt herself blush a little. Was he teasing her? She flicked him a faintly defensive sideways glance. 'I thought horses were supposed to be your area of expertise? I'm not so sure I should be feeling flattered.'

'Horses and wine and women. I have three areas of expertise. And I would say that you, my dear Liza Blake, are an extremely fine example of the last one. A really extremely fine example indeed.'

Of course. How could she have forgotten? He was a ladies' man. A Don Juan. An expert in the arts of flattery and seduction. And for a moment, Liza was torn. Should she deliver him a cold look, just to let him know she wasn't on the menu? Or should she take this opportunity to resume her own strategy of seduction?

But it felt a little too dangerous to do the latter. So, steering a safer middle course, she smiled and swivelled round to face him. 'Is this some kind of English chat-up?' she challenged.

But the smile was dying on her face even before she had finished the question. The look in his eyes was making her heart shiver and causing a tingle of expectation to rush down her spine. Suddenly, she rather liked the idea of being on the menu, after all.

Very slowly, Richard was shaking his head. 'It's not a chat-up, sweet Liza. It's simply the truth.'

Then, very gently, he was drawing her closer, slipping both his arms around her waist. And as Liza felt his hard warmth press against her, a great liquid wave of pleasure filled her. Her hands fluttered to his shoulders. With a sigh, she sank against his chest.

For a moment their eyes met and melted into each other. It was a moment that seemed to stretch to infinity. And then, making her sigh, Richard bent to kiss her.

This isn't happening. I must be dreaming this. Any minute now I'm going to wake up.

In a kind of dreamy, half-hearted protest these words kept circling round and round in Liza's head. For it must be a dream. She would not have let this happen. How could it be that she was standing here kissing Richard Hawkes?

For that was precisely what she was doing. It wasn't just him who was doing the kissing. As his lips closed over hers, Liza kissed him back eagerly, every inch of her burning and throbbing with desire.

It was a glorious feeling. One hand fluttered to his shoulder, while the other reached up lightly to touch his hair, that felt as soft and slippery as silk beneath her fingers. As he drew her even closer, she sighed and shuddered.

One hand was reaching for her breast, moulding it softly, sending fierce darts of longing shooting through her. Liza clung to him hungrily, aware through her excitement that she had never felt anything even remotely like this before. And she could not fight it. She might as well have fought a tidal wave.

'See how well the Hawkeses and the Blakes can get on when they try?' As Richard kissed her ear lobe, she felt him smile. Then he came round to kiss her lips again and looked into her eyes. 'And, surely you must agree, this is much nicer than fighting?'

It was odd, but Liza felt no awkwardness at all, as she continued to stand there, her hands curled around his shoulders, as naturally as though she had been like this with him all her life.

She smiled back at him. 'I wouldn't argue with that.'

'So, it looks like a truce, then?' Richard bent to kiss her nose.

Liza nodded and smiled at him, not quite daring to kiss him back, though she longed to do so with every ounce of her being. Then suddenly a thought struck her. 'Does that mean that you believe me? I mean about having nothing to do with those awful letters?'

'I guess it does, more or less. Ninety-nine point nine per cent.' He kissed her again, his lips lingering over hers. 'I've decided to let you talk me into believing you for the moment.' He drew back a little, dark eyes twinkling. 'In fact, I've decided to let you talk me into anything you like.'

'That might prove dangerous.'

'I'm prepared to take that risk.' He kissed her again, softly. Then with a reluctant sigh he began to draw away from her. 'But I'm afraid we're going to have to wait until a little later for you to have your wicked way with me.' He smiled and took her hands in his and kissed her fingers one by one. 'Alas, for the moment, duty calls. I have a couple of important phone calls to make.'

Then he held her eyes, making her breath catch as he added, 'But, not to worry. We have the rest of the weekend.'

They were standing apart now as he released her hands at last, but Liza still felt as though she was pressed against him. The sweet virile warmth of him continued to embrace her. The scent of him still tingled in her nostrils. She felt as bound to him as though they were two halves of a circle, or the Siamese twins he had once threatened they would become.

He smiled, still holding her eyes. 'How does that sound?'

Liza could feel her heart dancing. 'It sounds fine,' she agreed.

For a long moment they continued to gaze at one another. How has this happened? Liza was asking herself in wonder. I've never felt so light-headed and perfectly happy in my life!

But it was at that precise moment that the rug was snatched from under her.

For, suddenly, there was a movement in the doorway behind them, and in perfect unison with Richard she was turning towards it. And there, standing smiling at her, clearly delighted to see her and clearly expecting an equally delighted response from her, was someone whose existence she had entirely forgotten.

Liza felt herself freeze.

'Elliott!' she gasped.

CHAPTER SIX

'WELL, now, this is an unexpected pleasure!'

As Liza continued to stand there, stiff and immobile, blinking at Elliott, who still stood in the doorway as though he were some kind of apparition, Richard was stepping forward, one hand extended, to greet him.

'Pleased to meet you,' he said. 'I'm Richard Hawkes. You must be the boyfriend Liza's been telling me about?'

Elliott looked a little nonplussed. 'I hope I'm not interrupting. Your housekeeper said you were probably here...' Then he broke off and held out his hand politely. 'Yes,' he said. 'I'm Elliott Cramer.'

As Liza watched the scene, marvelling at Richard's composure, she was hurriedly gathering herself together. Which was not an easy task. In that moment when she'd glanced up and seen Elliott standing in the drawing-room doorway she'd almost fallen to the floor in disbelief and horror.

What had she been playing at with Richard a moment ago? Shame on her! She had entirely forgotten about Elliott!

'Elliott! It's great to see you!' Rapidly recovering, she was hurrying across the room to greet him, hugging him warmly and reaching up to kiss him. 'Why didn't you let me know you were coming?'

'I wanted to surprise you.'

As he kissed her back, Liza clung to him, seeking sanity in the familiar feel of his embrace. She buried her face against his shoulder, reluctant to release him. 'Well, you certainly did that—but I can't think of a nicer surprise!'

'Liza and I were just planning our weekend.' Richard spoke now, his tone touched with wry amusement. 'Strictly work, you understand. No rest for the wicked.'

'So, you're not going to be free?' Elliott glanced down at Liza, disappointed. Then he turned his gaze on Richard with a flicker of disapproval. 'I must say, that sounds a little excessive to me. I would have thought you'd at least let her have the weekend free.'

'Not when there's work to do, I'm afraid. And at a racing stables at this time of year there's always work to do.' Richard's tone was light, but oddly challenging, as he added, 'Don't worry. Liza understands. You won't catch her complaining.'

It was true, Liza hadn't complained when he'd told her she had to work today. For one thing, she'd been thinking she'd be gone by tomorrow, anyway! But there had been something about that remark of his that had grated a little. He'd somehow managed to hint at some mutually dedicated partnership that very definitely excluded Elliott. And he had no business to go suggesting such things.

Liza cast him a quick scowl to let him know she was annoyed, then turned with a placatory smile to Elliott. 'Don't worry, I'll be off this evening,' she told him. 'That's no problem. We can have dinner together.'

As she spoke, she was still holding on to Elliott's arm, which it struck her was not something she would normally be doing. Normally, she and Elliott were not overly physical. They didn't go in for hand-holding and displays of affection.

But she felt a need to do so now out of simple loyalty. For she had sensed, ever so subtly, a clash of discord between the two men. In spite of the hand-shaking and outward politeness, they hadn't taken to one another one tiny iota—and she wanted it in no doubt with which of the two her loyalties lay.

Richard was glancing at his watch. 'I'll leave you two now. I have a couple of quick phone calls to make.' Then he glanced at Elliott. 'What are your plans, if I may ask?'

Elliott shrugged uncertainly. 'I have no plans, really. I'd rather been banking on Liza being free. But since she's clearly not, I'll probably just go back to my hotel.' He shrugged. 'Never mind, it's a nice day for a walk.'

'You don't have a car, then?'

'No, I came here by cab.'

Richard narrowed his eyes. 'In that case,' he told the other man, 'I'll see to it that one of my men gives you a lift back.'

'No, really. Don't bother. I'd prefer to walk.'

But Richard was already swivelling round to address Liza. 'Be ready and waiting outside in the courtyard in ten minutes. You and I have some speed trials to do down at the practice track.'

'I know. I hadn't forgotten,' Liza assured him a little tightly. As she spoke, she continued to hold on to Elliott's arm.

'Good.' Richard's tone was equally tight. 'Ten minutes,' he said again. 'Don't keep me waiting.' Then he turned with a grim smile and marched out of the room.

It was only once Richard had gone that Liza released Elliott's arm. But not before she had reached up to give him another quick kiss.

'It really is terrific to see you,' she told him.

'It's terrific to see you, too. You're looking great, Liza.' Then he frowned. 'I just wish I were able to stay longer, especially since you seem to have so little time free. But I'm afraid this is just a flying visit. I have to go back to London tomorrow. I have some papers I have to prepare for an important meeting on Monday.'

'Never mind. We have this evening. We can go out for a meal.'

But Elliott was still frowning. 'Does he always work you this hard? I mean it's three o'clock on a Saturday afternoon and here you are, still slaving away.'

'Yes, I'm afraid he does.' Liza pulled a face. She'd been about to add that in a way she didn't mind, that to her surprise she actually found the work quite enjoyable, but she sensed that might not be the right thing to say. So, instead, she joked, 'You're the one to speak! You're planning to spend Sunday working!'

'Yes, but I'm not supposed to be on holiday. You came here for a holiday, Liza, not to be driven like some slave.'

'I know, I know. And this is definitely no holiday.' That was one point she certainly couldn't argue with. 'But don't worry, I won't be staying on much longer.' She winked at him. 'If all goes well, I might even be able to leave tomorrow.'

'Really? That's terrific.' Elliott looked delighted. 'In that case, throw away your train ticket. You're coming back with me. When I get back to my hotel I'll book you a seat on my flight.'

'No... Wait to do that. It's still not definite...' Then, as Elliott frowned, she added, 'I'll know definitely by this evening.' She glanced at her watch. 'I think I'd better go now. I don't want to keep the slave-driver waiting.'

As it turned out, it was Liza who ended up waiting—nearly fifteen minutes—for Richard. She was pacing up and down, fists clenched in annoyance, when he finally appeared without a word of apology.

All he said was, 'You should have waited in the Range Rover. The door was open. You didn't need to stand about in the courtyard.' Then, unhurriedly, ignoring her fuming expression, he climbed on board and switched on the engine.

Liza climbed up into the passenger seat and slammed the door shut behind her. 'Was that deliberate?' she demanded. 'Did you tell me ten minutes because you knew you were going to be more than twice as long?'

'And why would I do that?' As he released the handbrake, Richard turned to flick her an unrepentant smile. 'Anyway, what difference does it make? Ten minutes here or there, surely, don't matter? You'll have all evening with your boyfriend.'

That flippant remark with its cynical overtones seemed to confirm what Liza had already been suspecting.

She accused him, 'You did it to break us up and get Elliott out of here, didn't you? The same reason you laid on your instant escort agency!' Her tone was laced with the irritation that filled her. 'Go on! Admit it! That's what you were doing.'

They were heading down the road that led to the stables now, leaving the sunlit castle behind. 'Escort agency?' Richard flicked a glance at her, feigning a look of total incomprehension—though Liza could tell from the twinkle of amusement in his eyes that he understood precisely what she was getting at. 'What sort of escort agency are you talking about?'

Liza flicked a glance back at him. 'You know what I'm meaning! Just as Elliott and I were about to leave the house, Jim turned up on the doorstep in the van, absolutely insisting on your say-so that he take Elliott back to his hotel immediately. In spite of the fact,' she added angrily, 'that Elliott had told you he'd prefer to walk. You couldn't have made it any plainer that you didn't want him around!'

Richard simply shrugged. 'And did Elliott accept Jim's lift?'

'Sure he did. He had no choice.'

'Of course he had a choice. He could have said no. If someone offered me a lift I didn't want, I'd say no.' His eyes swivelled round for a moment to fix her. 'And so, I very much suspect, would you.'

'Maybe. But Elliott's different.'

She did not look back at him. What he was saying was perfectly true, but she didn't like the implication. He was hinting again, just as he had earlier, at some trait they shared that excluded Elliott.

Defending Elliott, she added, 'Elliott's polite.'

'Well, all I can say is he couldn't have been too keen on walking. It seems to me that by offering him a lift I was just doing him a favour. I know how you townies hate to walk.'

They were turning off the road now and into the area around the paddock, where Thunder was waiting, already saddled up. At the sound of the Range Rover, the black horse turned round expectantly, pricked up his ears and gave a little whinny.

And, through her anger, Liza couldn't help smiling. That silly horse really loves Richard, she thought.

But before that thought had a chance to soften her anger, she turned accusing eyes on Richard again. 'What were you so frightened of anyway,' she put to him hotly, 'that you couldn't bear to leave us alone for an extra ten minutes? What did you think was going to happen that you had to have him escorted off the premises instantly?'

Richard had pulled on the handbrake and now he turned to look at her. His expression was mocking as he told her,

'Maybe I was afraid that, as soon as I was out of the room, you would drag him to the floor and make passionate love to him. And I couldn't risk that. You might have damaged the carpet. And it happens to be a rather valuable Qum.'

Liza blinked at that, her cheeks flushing scarlet. This was not the way she had expected the conversation to turn.

'Well, you looked as though you might,' Richard added, still watching her as she continued to blink at him in consternation. 'The way you were insisting on hanging all over him it seemed highly likely. In fact, I was a little concerned at one point that you might not wait until I'd gone.'

'You're just being crude and ridiculous!' Liza found her tongue. 'I was doing no such thing!'

'Of course, I know I've really only got myself to blame.' Richard continued to look at her, dark eyes taunting. 'After all, I'd done a pretty good job of warming you up before he arrived.'

Liza's poor cheeks were almost on fire now.

'I don't know what the devil you're talking about,' she stuttered, suddenly wishing she'd never started this benighted conversation. 'I was just pleased to see him, that's all,' she added lamely. Suddenly, she couldn't quite manage to look him in the eye.

'I agree that you certainly seemed pleased to see him.' She could feel Richard's dark eyes boring into her. 'As I said, I was really quite seriously worried you might drag him down on to the carpet right there before my eyes.' He paused just a beat before adding in an amused tone, 'The very same carpet that just a few moments before you'd been on the point of dragging *me* down on to.'

'Don't kid yourself!' Liza's eyes darted up at that. 'I can assure you that nothing was ever further from my mind!'

'Really?' He was smiling a dismissively amused smile. 'As the saying goes, you could have fooled me.'

'Then you must be easily fooled.'

Liza was fighting her hardest to look as though she meant what she was saying. For, though it appalled her now to remember what had passed between them, she could remember what it had felt like all too clearly. And though his tasteless gibe concerning her and the Qum carpet was very definitely a bit of an exaggeration, it wasn't as big an exaggeration as she might have wished. There had been desire in her loins. Fierce and real.

He regarded her cynically. 'Is that how you do things? Get one man to warm you up and another one to finish you off?'

That was crude and uncalled for.

'How dare you speak to me like that?' As anger flooded through her, Liza reacted automatically and lunged across at him, one hand raised to strike him. 'No one speaks to me like that and gets away with it!'

'No? And I'm afraid no one gets away with trying to hit me.' Long before her hand could make contact with his face, Richard had caught her swiftly by the wrist, his fingers closing tightly, like a steel trap.

And now, the way he was holding her, Liza was lying half across him, her breasts pressed against his chest, her face inches from his.

'I won't hit you! Let me go! I didn't mean it!' she protested.

But he did not let her go. 'You haven't answered my question.'

'Did you really expect me to? There's nothing to answer!'

Liza's wrist was hurting, but that was not what was upsetting her. What was upsetting her was the way, in an effort to remain half upright, she was being forced to lean one hand against Richard's left thigh. She could feel the heat of the hard muscles burn right through her skin.

'Elliott's my boyfriend!' she insisted angrily, her eyes focusing anywhere but on Richard's. She knew it would be unwise to look into his eyes. She knew what always happened when she did.

'What happened earlier, between you and me, was nothing,' she protested. 'It was a mistake,' she went on, still not looking at him. 'I don't even know how it could have happened!'

'You don't know how it happened?' He was smiling, taunting her. And it seemed to Liza he was rather enjoying this whole situation.

'No, I'm afraid I don't!' If she removed her hand from his thigh, all that would happen was that she would end up falling right on top of him—unless she could get a grip of the seat instead. 'I must have taken leave of my senses.'

'Yes, I guess you must have.' He continued to hold her. Then he demanded, 'Do you take leave of your senses often?'

'As a matter of fact, I don't!'

Trying to straighten her spine, which wasn't at all easy in her current position, Liza made an effort to shift her weight from the hand on his thigh and move that hand to the edge of his seat.

But it was impossible. She couldn't do it. She would end up sprawling all over him. Losing patience and momentarily forgetting her determination not to look at him, she glared at him, tugging at the hand he still held. 'Will you stop playing stupid games with me and let me go?'

'I will. In a moment.'

His eyes seemed to coil round her, drawing her, bewitching her, just as she'd known they would. And suddenly all she knew was the wicked magic power of him and that she had not the strength within her to resist it.

Then he smiled. 'But first a small reminder, since you seem to require one, of what happened before.'

An instant later, he was kissing her before she could pull away from him, his lips sizzling against hers, making her heart race inside her. And at the hard warm sensuous touch of his lips, Liza momentarily felt her spirit fail her and was seized with a desire to just give in and kiss him back.

But though it took all of her strength, she managed to resist. Instead, taking advantage of the fact that as he bent to kiss her he had slackened his grip around her wrist, with a surge of determined strength Liza snatched herself free, pulling away from him and falling back in her seat again.

Her eyes blazed across at him. 'You're a pig!' she spat.

'I'm just keeping you warm for Elliott. Doing you both a favour.' Richard simply laughed in the face of her insult. 'After all, it'll be a few hours till you're back together again. I wouldn't want you cooling down in the meantime.'

'You're vile.' Liza glared at him. 'As I said before, I really don't know how what happened could have happened.' She held up a warning hand

just in case he had in mind another little demon-
stration. 'I didn't just take leave of my senses. I
must have been stark, staring crazy.'

'Yes, you were pretty crazy. Lucky Elliott.'
Richard subjected her for a moment to a deep, un-
hurried scrutiny. 'Do you get crazy like that with
Elliott?'

Liza threw him a furious look. 'I won't even
answer that. In fact, I'm surprised you had the bad
taste to ask it. Though I suppose I shouldn't be.'
Her eyes tore into him. 'As you keep demon-
strating, there's really no limit to your bad taste.'

The accusation just slid off him. 'As I said, lucky
Elliott.' Then, at last, with a small shrug, he detached his gaze from hers and reached out to push
open the driver's door. 'I think it's time we got
down to some work.'

The next moment, to Liza's relief, they were
climbing out of the car. She took a deep breath,
carefully keeping her distance as she followed
Richard across to the paddock. Then she smiled as
Thunder whinnied and came to the gate to greet
him.

'Hello, there, my beauty. How are you doing?'
Richard stroked the horse's neck as it nuzzled his
shoulder. 'How do you feel about going for a ride?'

Liza watched beneath her lashes. With his horses
he was an angel. No one could fault him in the way
he treated his horses. He was their master, yet
he treated them almost as equals. And all of
them, and especially Thunder, quite obviously
adored him.

He was climbing into the saddle and leading the big stallion out of the paddock and on to the practice racecourse.

'I just want you to do the usual,' he told Liza across his shoulder, as she followed on foot close behind him. 'Just make a note of the times for each circuit we do. I want to see if he's continuing to make progress.'

Liza had done this before and it was a job she enjoyed doing. 'Right,' she nodded, climbing up into the observer's chair that was positioned with an unrestricted view out over the track. She reached for the stop watch and notepad and pencil that were kept in a built-in cupboard under the seat.

'Ready whenever you are,' she told him.

Richard was ready to go, riding crop in hand. But suddenly he paused and turned to look at Liza.

'You know, I wasn't really worried that you might seduce your lover and in the process make a mess of my beautiful Qum carpet...'

As she flushed, he paused and deliberately held her eyes. 'And the reason I wasn't worried is because I happen to know that the only man you'll ever make love with on that carpet is me.'

Then, leaving her speechless and fumbling for the button of her stop watch, with a twitch of the reins he was galloping off down the racecourse.

In the end, they spent a good hour down at the practice track, with Liza faithfully recording each lap time in her notebook. Each lap time, that was, except the first one. In her astonishment, she'd made a bit of a hash of that. But all the others she'd recorded faithfully and accurately.

'He's doing well,' she was able to tell Richard each time he stopped by to check. 'He's managing to keep his time pretty steady, and it's an improvement on the last set of times in the book.'

But, in spite of her diligence, Liza was finding it hard to concentrate.

What was that last remark about the Qum carpet supposed to mean? she kept asking herself, over and over, as she watched him. Was it just one of his tasteless jokes, or had he actually been serious? Had he meant it as some sort of perverted warning? And where did he get the nerve to make a comment like that, anyway?

It's my own fault, she told herself. It was that kiss in the drawing-room. In a moment of madness I gave him an inch and now he thinks he can take a mile. Look at what had happened in the Range Rover just a short while ago! The things he had said...the way he had tried to kiss her again...! It was scandalous and there was no way she would stand for any more of it!

Though, at least, there'd been no repeats over the past sixty minutes. His behaviour had been impeccable and the few words they'd exchanged had been strictly related to the business in hand. It was as though he'd never made that uncouth suggestion about the Qum carpet.

But he had and, in spite of herself, Liza couldn't stop thinking about it, as through narrowed eyes she gazed out over the track at the lean muscular figure glued to Thunder's back, a picture of grace and elegance and power. The damned impudent nerve of him! she kept muttering.

Though what did it matter? she told herself crossly. Why should she even think twice about his impudence? She'd been lured into that first kiss, but there would be no repetitions. Elliott was her man. It was Elliott she wanted. And it was Elliott she would be hurrying back to London to be with, just as soon as Richard had shown her the ballroom.

She certainly didn't want Richard Hawkes, she told herself, in spite of the way she sometimes couldn't help reacting to him. She was hardly likely to want a man, who on his own admission, was only interested in the chase!

Liza was soothing herself with this thought when at last Richard came trotting up to her.

'I think that's enough for now. Let's call it a day,' he was saying. 'I reckon Thunder could probably go another few laps, but then he's a few years younger than me.'

As he spoke, he smiled and affectionately pulled the horse's ears. Thunder whinnied and tossed his black head in response.

Liza smiled back at him, touched as she always was by the warmth that existed between him and the black stallion. 'Well, I have to say,' she told him, 'he looked pretty terrific out there. He looked as though nothing in the world could beat him.'

As she said it, she reached out to stroke Thunder's warm soft muzzle, something that just a few days ago she would never have dreamed of doing, she reflected. But she was almost sorry she'd done it as her eyes met Richard's. She could see from his smile that he'd been thinking the same.

He threw her a wink. 'My goodness me. Is this really the townie from Philadelphia who used to be afraid of horses?' Then, before she could answer, he was turning away. 'Let's go. After all, you've got a big night tonight. No doubt you'll want a couple of hours to get yourself ready for Elliott.'

Liza slid down from her chair, scowling at him as she did so. He thought he was so smart. He thought he knew everything. He thought he understood her. But he didn't.

In a clipped tone, she pointed out to him, 'I won't need a couple of hours. There'll be plenty of time for you to show me the ballroom—which, I seem to remember, is what you promised.'

'I said I *might* show you the ballroom tonight. I certainly didn't make any promises.' Richard tossed her a quick glance over his shoulder. 'And in the circumstances I've decided we ought to postpone that. At least, until your boyfriend has gone back to London.'

'But that's not fair!' As he began to head for the stables, Liza hurried on foot behind him. 'That's not fair!' she protested again. 'You could easily show me it this evening!'

'But I'm not going to.' He couldn't have cared less about the fairness of it. 'So, that's that, and you needn't waste your time making a song and dance about it.'

And, with that, he proceeded to change the subject.

'At least you and Elliott,' he was saying in that mocking tone he always seemed to use when he mentioned Elliott, 'will have plenty to talk about over dinner tonight. You can tell him all about your growing love of horses.'

Liza glared at his back with irritation. He had told her there was no point in making a song and dance and she could tell he was absolutely serious about that. She could try to fight him all she liked. He would not be budged.

She wondered fleetingly if it was worth trying to wheedle him round, but rejected the idea more or less instantly. Quite frankly, she had rather lost her taste for wheedling. For one thing, it was potentially far too dangerous and for another she was too angry even to pretend to be nice to him. For it looked as though she wouldn't be leaving tomorrow, after all.

In a flinty tone she responded to that last remark of his. 'Elliott and I *always* have plenty to talk about. But I shouldn't think he'll be interested in hearing about horses. He'll be more interested in telling me about what he's been up to in London. Theatres and things. That's what Elliott and I have in common.'

'That's a pity. In that case, you won't be able to share with him all the progress you've made over the past few days here.' Surprising her, Richard turned round to deliver a look of approval. 'For you have, you know. You've done exceptionally well.

'But never mind,' he added with an irritating wink, 'Even if Elliott doesn't, *I* appreciate what you've achieved.'

Then, with a snap of the reins, he proceeded to trot ahead of her, leaving Liza fulminating black looks at his back, yet not quite sure why that remark had made her so mad.

* * *

Liza did not, as Richard had mockingly suggested, spend hours getting ready for her dinner date with Elliott that evening.

Richard understood nothing, she told herself with satisfaction, as she slipped on a pair of blue cotton trousers and a simple blue and cream patterned blouse and pulled a comb through her pale auburn hair. She and Elliott did not have the kind of relationship where each was out to impress the other.

They had an informal relationship, without frills or fuss. Liza wouldn't have dreamed of dressing up for a dinner date with Elliott, and Elliott would have been astonished if she had!

They went to a quaint little restaurant called Nellie's Kitchen and ordered steaks with salad and a bottle of the house red. And it was so nice, Liza kept telling herself, to be with him again. Elliott was easy company. There was no tension between them, like there always was between her and Richard, no sense of somehow always being poised on the edge.

As she'd predicted, their conversation centred for the most part on what Elliott had been up to for the past few days. And Liza was quite happy to listen to his chatter about London. It kept irritating thoughts of Richard at bay.

Almost in spite of herself, however, she did slip in at one point, 'And, while you've been doing all that, I've been learning about race horses.'

As soon as she'd said it, though, she wished she hadn't.

'Learning about race horses? Whatever next!'

Elliott's dismissive response came as no surprise, but her own reaction to it did. Just for a flickering instant, she felt disappointed and annoyed. Secretly, she'd been hoping he'd ask her to elaborate. But there was no chance of that. The subject had been dropped. He was already going on to tell her, as he cut into his steak,

'Work's really been pretty hectic this past week, but, thank heavens, mid-week, I managed to get to a concert. It was at the Albert Hall. You would have loved it.'

'I'll bet I would.' Liza smiled back at him, forgiving him. Hadn't she known he wouldn't be interested in silly horses? And neither would she once she got back to London and civilisation! She leaned across the table towards him. 'What was the programme?' she invited him to tell her.

Elliott was only too happy to tell her in detail. 'But, don't worry,' he concluded, as she pulled an envious face at him. 'There's another equally good concert on next week. If you like, I can get tickets for both of us.'

'Oh, Elliott, I'd love to, but——'

'But what, Liza?' Elliott laid down his cutlery and frowned across at her, as he proceeded to renew the argument he'd made at the beginning of the evening. 'Surely you must know you're going to get nowhere with that man? He's never going to show you the ballroom. He's just wasting your time. He's just roped you in on false pretences to do a load of menial jobs, that quite frankly are beneath you. He's just using you, Liza. Can't you see that?'

'Yes, you're probably right.' Liza stared gloomily at the tablecloth, remembering her last exchange with Richard on the subject. 'I must say I'm beginning to think that myself.'

'Then do as I suggest. Come back with me.' Elliott cast her a sympathetic glance across the table. 'I saw your old flatmate the other day. She said your old room's ready and waiting. So there's no problem about where to stay in London. And your Aunt Julia will understand. You've done your best. No one, after all, can ask more than that.'

Liza nodded. 'You're probably right—though I hate to let Aunt Julia down.' Then she sighed. 'But what can I do against a wretched man like that? I think you're right. He's just not going to co-operate.'

'So leave. Right away. Come back with me tomorrow. Tell Hawkes what to do with his job. Working in that place is no good for you.'

The more she listened to him, the more sensible his advice was sounding. Tonight had been such a civilised oasis. This was where she belonged—here with Elliott, with a man who shared her back-ground and who understood her. A man who en-joyed the things that she enjoyed, and who respected her and cared for her.

And suddenly it seemed so obvious she won-dered why on earth she was hesitating.

She looked across at Elliott. 'OK,' she told him. 'When I go back tonight, I'll tell Richard I'm leaving. I'll go back with you on that flight tomorrow.'

CHAPTER SEVEN

And so, it was all settled.

Liza climbed into her taxi, after bidding Elliott goodnight with a kiss, and smiled as he told her, 'I'll pick you up about ten. We'll be back in London around lunchtime.'

That's a relief, she told herself, as the taxi door slammed shut and the driver headed for Abbotsdale Castle. This would be her last night in Yorkshire. Her last night at the castle. And her last night anywhere near the obnoxious Richard Hawkes.

She sat back in her seat. The only real regret she had was that she wouldn't be taking back any pictures of the ballroom for Aunt Julia.

Though, that wasn't quite so. She glanced out at the darkened landscape. She also deeply regretted having to leave Yorkshire so soon. This beautiful land of her forebears had rather got under her skin. Saying goodbye to it would be a bit of a wrench.

It would also be a bit of a wrench saying goodbye to the castle, she found herself thinking, somewhat to her own surprise. It would even be a little sad taking her farewell of the horses—and Jim and Penny and the rest of the staff.

In fact, the more she thought about it the only part she had no qualms about was finally saying goodbye to Richard. And that should more than make up for all the rest, she told herself. As far as she was concerned, Richard was definitely bad news.

Liza was so lost in these thoughts that, as the taxi approached the castle, at first she didn't notice anything strange.

But then suddenly she leaned forward. What was going on? All the castle lights were blazing, yet none of the curtains was drawn and the big oak door was standing wide open.

And, as she frowned, suddenly anxious, she was all at once aware of a strange, frightening electricity crackling in the air. In that moment, instinctively, she knew something was wrong.

'Here!' Not wasting a moment, she reached into her bag and pulled out a banknote to pay off the driver. 'Thanks,' she told him, barely waiting to take her change from him before jumping impatiently out of the car.

Then she was rushing across the courtyard and only missed by a hair's breadth colliding with Richard who'd just come running out through the open door.

As he sprinted past her, heading for the Range Rover that was parked in its usual place in a corner of the courtyard, Liza hurried breathlessly after him. 'What's going on? Is something wrong? Has something happened?' she wanted to know.

Richard didn't even glance at her, but from the set look on his face it was obvious that there was something very wrong indeed.

'The stables are on fire. I've just had a phone call.' His tone was as steely as the look on his face. He let out an oath. 'Pray God the fire brigade gets here soon.'

'The stables? On fire?' Liza was panting with the effort of keeping up with him, as he reached the parked Range Rover and yanked the door open. Then, as he jumped inside and switched on the engine, she was running round to the other side of the car. 'Wait for me! I'm coming with you!'

Needless to say, he didn't bother to wait, and the car was already moving as Liza scrambled aboard. She hauled the door shut behind her and held on tight to her seat as they swung out of the courtyard and on to the road to the stables.

And it suddenly struck her, as she glanced across at Richard, who still hadn't looked once in her direction, that perhaps he believed she had something to do with this tragedy. After all, she'd been out of his sight all evening—and he'd admitted to still having doubts about her involvement with these threatening letters.

He'd said he believed in her innocence ninety-nine point nine per cent. That still left room for a grain of suspicion to grow.

It was a chilling thought. Liza turned to face his scowling profile and told him quietly, 'I had nothing to do with this. I promise you.'

Richard didn't answer. In fact, he may not even have heard her. For suddenly, at last, the stables had come into view and every atom of his attention was fixed on the scene before them.

At first sight the stables appeared to have been reduced to a raging holocaust. Liza felt herself freeze. 'Oh, no!' she breathed in horror, her thoughts flying in a rush of desperate fear to the animals who were trapped inside. Surely, none of them could have survived!

But, as they drew closer, she could see that, though quite bad enough, the fire was not yet out of control. There was really only one end of the stables that had been affected so far—though it was the end where Richard's beloved Thunder was stabled.

And then they were swinging to a halt and Richard was leaping out.

'All we can do for the moment is concentrate on getting the horses to safety. There's no point in wasting time trying to put out the fire. The fire brigade can do that when they get here.'

Richard pointed to a section of building where the fire still hadn't reached. 'You start there, and I'll start over here.' Then he was sprinting over to the corner where the fire raged most fiercely.

Liza didn't waste a moment in doing as he'd told her. He was right. The first thing they had to do was save the horses. And, thank heavens, at the end of the stables where she'd been sent, the animals, though badly frightened, were all unharmed. Without any difficulty, she was able to lead them out of their stalls and corral them in the nearby paddock, out of harm's way.

'You're OK,' she told them, stroking their muzzles comfortingly. But what, she wondered fearfully, had become of Thunder?

The fire brigade arrived in a matter of minutes, just as the last of the horses was being led to safety. And in no time at all fire hoses were being mounted and the raging chaos of a short while ago was rapidly being brought under control.

Through the busy, disciplined throng of uniformed firemen, Liza went to look for Richard—

and tracked him down at last at the back of the burnt-out shell that once had been Thunder's stable. Now it resembled nothing so much as a blackened, burnt-out oven.

She looked up into his face that, behind the smears of dirt, she could see was drawn and as pale as paper. 'Where is he?' she asked. There was no need to say she meant Thunder.

Richard said nothing for a moment, then he shrugged a painful shrug. 'This was the first part of the stables to go, I'm afraid. Nothing inside here could have survived . . .'

He cast a painful eye at the wreckage at his feet— the blackened timbers of the roof that lay in a charred, smouldering heap, the still-smoking tiles that had turned to rubble.

'Nothing in here could have survived,' he said again.

As he spoke, his features were torn with a look of such terrible grief that Liza felt the tears fly to her eyes. Unable to speak, she too stared helplessly at the ground. Somewhere under that wreckage Thunder must be buried.

Then she reached out her hand to him. 'I'm so sorry,' she whispered, for she could guess at the pain that tore at his heart.

He did not look at her, but he caught her hand in his and held it tightly for a moment. Then they just stood there silently, united in sorrow, understanding without words what the other was feeling. It seemed to Liza they were the only two people in the world.

But then, breaking the spell, there was a sudden movement behind them, accompanied by a soft, familiar whinny.

The two of them swung round as one, scarcely daring to believe what they were hearing. But it was no hallucination. They hadn't been hearing things. For there before them, as big and as beautiful as ever, stood a faintly nervous-looking, but quite unharmed, Thunder.

'He's OK!'

Overjoyed, Liza turned to glance at Richard and felt her heart twist at the relief and joy in his face. His pallor had gone and he was smiling broadly as the big horse gently nuzzled his shoulder.

'You old devil! Where have you been?' He pulled the horse's ears affectionately. 'Don't you know you nearly gave me a heart attack?'

'He must have got out.' Liza, too, was beaming broadly. She stroked the horse's shoulder. 'Thank heavens for that!'

'He must have kicked the door down when the fire started. I thought there might be a small chance of that, but I didn't really dare to hope.' For the first time, Richard turned to look at Liza squarely. 'I must say, you look almost as relieved as I feel.'

'I am. I couldn't have borne for anything to have happened to Thunder.' As she said it, it struck Liza there was too much emotion in her voice. She felt the need to add hastily, 'Or to any of the other horses. I would have hated it if any of them had got hurt.'

'You really have grown fond of them.'

Richard smiled as he said it and held her eyes with that penetrating look he had that seemed to reach down into her soul. But, for once, Liza had no trouble admitting he was right.

'Yes, I have,' she confessed. 'Very fond indeed.'

Richard continued to hold her eyes and there was softness in his expression, an intimacy of affection reaching out to her. It felt rather like that moment when he had taken her hand in his.

Then he winked at her. 'That's good,' he said. 'I think they've grown rather fond of you.' With a smile, he turned his attention back to Thunder. 'Let's get you into the paddock with the others,' he told the stallion. 'We've got quite a bit of clearing up to do here.'

The clearing up, in fact, took them into the small hours. Long after the fire brigade and the police had finally departed, they were tidying up with brooms and shovels and hoses the mess of mud and ashes and water—just enough so that they could house the animals for the night.

But at least they had an army of willing helpers. Jim and Ken, and all the other stable lads and girls, had appeared out of nowhere to lend a hand, and even a small posse of neighbours turned out to help. Still, it was past two a.m. when a thoroughly weary Liza climbed up into the Range Rover beside Richard for the short drive back to the castle.

'Straight to bed for you, my girl.' Richard cast a sympathetic glance at her. 'And, thanks,' he told her. 'You've really been a great help.'

'There's no need to thank me.' Liza shrugged off his gratitude. 'I only did what any decent person would do.' Then she paused and glanced at him, remembering what she'd told him earlier and how he still hadn't said whether he believed her or not.

'I hope you realise,' she added in an emphatic tone, 'that I had nothing to do with starting that fire? That's something I hope you're very clear about.'

'You said that before...'

Richard slanted a glance at her, and there was a flicker of something deep in his eyes that caused Liza to insist, 'And you do know it's true?' Surely, she thought appalled, he couldn't have any doubts?

But then he shook his head. 'No, I know you weren't involved. Neither you nor your boyfriend Elliott. You were nowhere near the scene of the crime. The two of you were having dinner at Nellie's Kitchen.'

'Precisely,' Liza sighed. 'I just wanted to be quite sure——' Then she halted in mid-sentence and narrowed her eyes at him. 'How did *you* know where we were?'

They had reached the castle forecourt and Richard was pulling on the handbrake. 'Here we are,' he said. 'Home at last.'

But as he jumped down on to the cobbles, Liza wasn't about to be fobbed off. She jumped down, too, and hurried after him as he headed for the big stone entrance porch.

'How did you know,' she insisted, 'that Elliott and I went to Nellie's Kitchen?'

'Abbotsdale is a small place. It's extremely easy to know such things. And besides...' Richard paused as he pushed the door open and stood aside to let her pass. 'I knew Nellie's Kitchen was the sort of restaurant Elliott would choose.'

Liza paused in the hallway and delivered a searching look. 'Are you trying to tell me you just guessed that's where we were? Well, I don't believe you. You didn't guess. You knew.' She felt a flare of sudden anger as she confronted him. 'How did you know?' she demanded.

Richard looked quite unperturbed by her sudden inquisition. 'Look,' he told her, 'if it's all right with you, I'd like to relax for half an hour with a drink before I finally collapse into bed. If you want to join me, I'll be in the drawing-room. But before I do anything else, I must have a shower.'

'You could answer my question first. I'm sure it wouldn't take a minute.' Liza made a tentative move to step in front of him and block his way as he headed for the stairs.

But he simply shook his head as he swept unstoppably past her. 'No, I'm afraid the shower has to come first. Then, after that, we'll see what we shall see.'

By the time he'd finished the sentence he was halfway up the stairs.

Liza glared after him in annoyance. Why did he have to be so uncooperative? She didn't feel like wasting time with a drink. She just wanted an answer to her question and then to be able to flop into bed. Though he was right about one thing. A shower was a must.

Fifteen minutes later, as she was towelling herself dry, Liza was aware that her tiredness had miraculously vanished. It must be the effect of the shower, she reflected. It had temporarily wakened her up. So, maybe, after all, a relaxing drink in the drawing-room might not be such a bad idea. If she were to go straight to bed, she knew she wouldn't sleep.

She pulled on a pair of fresh jeans and a blue and white striped T-shirt, combed her damp hair and pushed her feet into a pair of sandals. Then a moment later she was making her way downstairs.

But as Liza stepped through the drawing-room doorway, she blinked in amazement. She hadn't expected the occasion to be quite as informal as this!

Richard was seated on one of the sofas, brandy glass in hand, and all he was wearing was a knee-length towelling robe.

'Ah, there you are.' He glanced up to smile at her. 'I took the liberty of pouring you a brandy.' He indicated the glass on the table in front of him. 'But if you'd prefer something else, just say the word.'

'No, brandy's fine.'

Liza hovered in the doorway, momentarily immobilised by the astonishing vision of his unclad legs and the generous triangle of tanned chest that was exposed above the neck of his blue towelling robe. What a wonderful body he had, she couldn't help thinking. But perhaps there was just a little too much of it on display!

Richard seemed to read her thoughts. His smile curled at the corners. 'Sorry about the state of undress,' he told her. 'But I'm afraid I couldn't be bothered getting dressed again.' He shrugged a small shrug. 'I didn't think you'd mind.'

'I don't. Of course I don't.' He must think her an idiot the way she was standing there blinking at him from the doorway as though she had never seen a half-dressed man before.

She stepped towards him with a smile. 'I shouldn't have bothered to get dressed again either.'

But, as soon as she'd said that, she wished she hadn't. She had a sudden vision, sharp and vivid, of the two of them sitting together in their bathrobes with nothing underneath but warm, newly showered flesh and total nakedness only a tug of a belt away.

The vision had caused her stomach to clench quite disgracefully and a shameful shiver of excitement had shot right through her. It must be exhaustion making me hallucinate, she told herself firmly, as she crossed the room and seated herself in the armchair opposite Richard, thoroughly thankful, after all, that she *had* taken the time to dress!

He was smiling across at her. 'So, how do you feel now?'

'I feel much better after a shower.'

She reached for her brandy glass, hoping she looked cooler than she felt. Now that she was closer and more or less on a level with him, she was even more conscious of all the acres of naked flesh—and of how absolutely enticingly splendid it all was.

'You were right,' she continued, struggling to keep her eyes on his face. 'I think we probably do need a drink to unwind.'

Not that he looked in the least as though he needed to unwind. He was sitting back casually against the cushions, perfectly at ease. She was the one who was all twisted into knots!

But he seemed unaware of the tension in her, or maybe just took it for tiredness. Smiling, he raised his glass in a toast. 'Here's to a good night's work,' he said.

Liza smiled in agreement and raised her own glass. 'Oh, yes, I'll definitely drink to that.'

'You did a great job.' Richard held her eyes as he said it. 'I'll always be grateful for what you did tonight.'

Liza took a sip of her brandy and savoured it for a moment, feeling its warmth gradually begin to relax her. 'I was more than happy to help. Thank heavens I was there.' She glanced across at him. 'What will happen to the stables now? Will you be able to repair the damage?'

'Most of it, I think. We may have to rebuild a bit. Tomorrow I'll get the builders in to have a proper look.' He took a mouthful of his drink. 'It's definitely a bit of a mess. We may need to fix up some temporary accommodation for the horses. But the important thing is that none of them was hurt.'

'That was a miracle.' Liza nodded with feeling and let her mind roam back over the momentous events of the night. Then she smiled. 'You know,' she told him, teasing him, 'I'll never forget that moment when you turned round and saw Thunder standing behind you. I really wish I'd had a camera.'

'You were almost as pleased as I was.'

'Yes, I suppose I was. I would have been devastated if he'd been hurt.' As he smiled at her, she felt again the flow of warmth and shared caring that had passed between them at the stables.

Then abruptly, almost guiltily, she dropped her gaze away. 'I would have been devastated,' she amended carefully, 'if *any* of the horses had been hurt.'

It was the same protest she'd made last time, back at the stables. And though there was no doubt it was true, it was also true, in spite of her efforts to deny it, that she would have been doubly devastated if anything had happened to Thunder.

That struck her as strange. Why should she care so much about Thunder? And perhaps it was a sudden need to push that question from her that prompted her suddenly to remember what she was here for. She wasn't here just to enjoy a relaxing drink with Richard. She was here to demand an answer to her question—the question she had temporarily forgotten all about.

Laying down her glass, she sat forward in her seat. 'How did you know that Elliott and I were at Nellie's Kitchen?' Then, before he could answer, she put forward her own theory. 'You weren't by any chance having us followed?'

He did not answer immediately. His eyes narrowed as he looked at her. Then he nodded. 'Yes. I was having you watched.'

Liza blinked at him in astonishment. In spite of her accusation, she somehow hadn't actually expected that he would say yes. Or perhaps she'd just been *hoping* that he wouldn't say yes.

'So, you weren't kidding,' she observed in a dry tone, 'when you said you still didn't trust me one hundred per cent?'

'No, I wasn't kidding. Though, in fact, I was only half serious.' Richard leaned forward as he offered his explanation, and there was a look of apology in his eyes. 'I'd more or less decided you were innocent . . . until, out of the blue, your boyfriend showed up. I decided, since he was an unknown quantity, that just to be on the safe side I'd better keep an eye on both of you.'

'How could you?' Liza felt consumed with hurt and betrayal. She sat forward in her seat, her eyes flashing angrily across at him. 'How could you believe that of me—that I could do a thing like that? How could you? Go on, tell me! How could you?'

'Liza, calm down.' Richard frowned as he looked across at her. 'I was wrong. I admit it. But I was worried. I knew these letters weren't phonies. All I was doing was just trying to protect my horses.'

'Protect them from me, you mean! What do you take me for? Some kind of disgusting, deranged assassin? I can hardly believe what I'm hearing!'

Angrily, shakily, she rose to her feet. 'Well, I'm sorry, but I'm not staying around to listen to your insults!'

'Liza, you're over-reacting.' As she glared her defiance at him, suddenly Richard had risen to his feet, too. He took a step towards her and spoke to her gently. 'Look, you're tired. We should never have got into this conversation. Not now. It's been such an emotional night.'

'No, I'm glad we got into it!' Liza scarcely knew what she was saying. Suddenly, she was trembling all over with emotion. 'Now I know exactly what you think of me! And I'm glad we've finally got that clear!'

'Liza, calm down. I don't think that of you. I've told you I was wrong. I've told you I apologise.' He reached out with both hands and caught her by the arms and held her for a moment at arm's length, looking down at her. 'I apologise. Do you understand? I know now I was wrong about you. Tonight you proved that beyond any doubt.'

'I could never have done that! I could never have hurt your horses!' The tears were standing in her eyes as she looked back at him. 'I care for your horses. Especially Thunder.'

'I know.' He smiled at her. 'I know. I know.' Then, before she could resist, he was drawing her into his arms.

Liza might not have resisted anyway, for suddenly she was reeling from a sudden, quite unexpected revelation. For in a flash she had understood what she had not understood before—why it was that her concern had mostly been for Thunder, and why she kept feeling the need to deny it.

It was because she knew just how much Richard loved the black stallion and what a terrible blow his loss would have been to him, and because she couldn't have borne for him to have suffered such a loss. It was for Richard's sake that she had been so concerned about Thunder.

The realisation was a little shocking. Why should she care about Richard? And there was something else, too, that was a little shocking. It was because of her foolish caring that she was so upset now.

There she'd been, anxiously worrying on his behalf, while he'd been thinking she was some kind of monster. She knew that shouldn't matter. But it did. And it hurt.

Coming to her senses a little, she strained against him as he held her. 'I'm OK now,' she muttered. 'You were right. I'm overtired.'

'You are. We both are. It's been a long night.'

In spite of her resistance, Richard continued to hold her, not tightly, but firmly, his arms wrapped round her, as though she were some overwrought child he was comforting.

And the warmth and sure strength of him was indeed profoundly comforting, Liza found herself thinking, as her breathing grew more even again and her body gradually relaxed against him. The gentle way he was holding her was like an emotional massage. She could feel all the tightness in her begin to melt away and a wonderful feeling of peace come over her. With a sigh she let her head drop down against his chest.

Liza was vaguely aware of something brushing her hair. She sensed it was his lips, but she did not draw away. She just stayed where she was and felt her arms drift upwards to form a light circle around his waist.

'Tomorrow,' he was saying, 'you'll take the day off. I think you should sleep at least until lunchtime. And then you can just have a lazy afternoon.'

Tomorrow? For some reason, the word triggered a question in her head. Wasn't there something about tomorrow that she was forgetting?

But all she said was, 'And what about you? Will you be having a lazy day, too?'

'Me? No. I suspect I'll have anything but.' As he spoke, his breath whispered softly across her scalp, sending delightful little tingles up and down her spine. 'I'll be busy at the stables, trying to sort out the mess.'

'In that case, I'll be there to help you. I want to do everything I can.' The circle of her arms had tightened a little. Beneath the towelling of his robe she could feel the firmness of his flesh.

'No, I don't think you should do that. I think my idea was best.'

Again, Liza felt a light pressure against her hair, and this time she smiled, quite certain it was his lips.

Then he added, 'I'll do the work. Just you get your beauty sleep. After all...' His lips brushed softly against her hair again. 'We must have you looking your best for Monday night.'

'Monday night?'

With a frown, Liza tilted her head to look at him. And, as she looked into his face, she was aware of a jolt inside her, as though something had prodded at her heart and knocked it slightly off balance.

She swallowed. 'What's happening on Monday night?'

'Have you forgotten about our dinner with Ivan and Emmeline?' Richard smiled. 'Hey, you really do need your bed.'

Liza tried to smile back at him, but she was finding smiling difficult. In the past few seconds she had suddenly become aware of the hard virile body beneath the blue towelling robe. Suddenly, he was no longer just a strong, gentle comforter. Suddenly, she was aware of his potent masculinity, of every hard sinew and muscle and bump of him against which her own body was so guilelessly pressed.

And then she remembered what it was she had forgotten about tomorrow.

A shaft of horror went through her. She had planned to tell him she was leaving. With Elliott. On the plane back to London.

Suddenly overcome with guilt and horror at herself, she parted her lips, about to tell him. But she had left it too late. The very next instant her lips were sealed as he bent to kiss her.

It was the gentlest, most seductive kiss you could imagine. No one could have resisted it, Liza told herself later. And at that moment, she certainly was incapable of doing so.

His mouth was warm and exciting as it brushed hers. And it was the gentleness of the kiss, the sheer fleeting magic of it that pinned Liza to the floor and knocked all resistance out of her.

Had he been less gentle, she would have pulled away from him. Had he held her more tightly, she would have struggled. And she would never have stood for it for one moment had his tongue been more probing or his hands more intimate.

As it was, there was nothing she could possibly object to. The tenderness of his embrace was delightful, overwhelming, his kiss so sweet it took her breath away. To resist would have been self-denying and silly.

So she did not resist. She just closed her eyes and floated in a kind of dreamy, magical bliss. And it felt quite lovely to be so close to him, drawn into this easy, natural intimacy.

After a moment he drew back a little, though still holding her, and smiled down at her. 'I forgot to ask you...' he said with a strange smile. 'How was your evening...before the fire?'

'My evening?'

'Your dinner at Nellie's Kitchen.'

'The dinner was very nice. Very pleasant.' She looked back into his eyes, sensing that didn't sound quite right. 'Very nice indeed,' she emphasised.

'Good. It's a nice place. I go there quite often.'

As he said it, he smiled and looked deep into her eyes, making his words somehow sound like an invitation. And it was quite involuntary. Liza found herself thinking how nice it would be to have dinner with him at Nellie's Kitchen.

That brought her up short. How could she think such a thing? The only man she should be thinking of having dinner with was Elliott. And, likewise, Elliott was the only man she should be embracing. What was going on with her? Was she crazy or something?

She unclasped her arms guiltily and took a step back. 'I'm going to bed now,' she said. 'I'm really very tired. In fact, I'm so tired I scarcely know what I'm doing.' She shrugged awkwardly as he released her, as though explaining away what had just happened. 'I'm just about out of my head with tiredness.'

'You must be.' He simply smiled an enigmatic smile, giving away nothing of what he was thinking—or of what he thought of her explanation. 'Off you go and sleep,' he told her. 'And do as I said. Take tomorrow off.'

'Yes, I will. In fact, I was planning to anyway. You see, there's something I forgot to tell you . . .'

She took a deep breath and hurried on before he could stop her, 'I'm leaving tomorrow. I'm going back to London with Elliott.' As she finally said it, her relief was enormous. 'There's absolutely no point in my staying on here any longer. So, that's it. I've decided. I'm leaving right away.'

'I see. Oh, well.' Richard showed no emotion. He simply shrugged. 'If that's what you've decided, I can't stop you.'

'No, you can't.' As though to prove it, Liza headed for the door. Suddenly, she felt she couldn't get away from him quick enough. 'So, that's it, I'm afraid. I probably won't see you again.'

'So it would seem.'

Richard stood and watched her go, his hands pushed into the pockets of his blue towelling robe. And it was only as she actually stepped out into the corridor that he added in a quiet tone, almost as though speaking to himself,

'That's a pity. As a kind of thank-you for all your help tonight, I was planning to show you round the ballroom.'

CHAPTER EIGHT

LIZA halted in the doorway. 'Do you really mean that? I'm afraid I'm a bit too tired for jokes.'

Richard smiled and eyed her with a twinkle of amusement. 'Would I joke about something so serious?' he teased her. 'Surely you know me better than that?'

'That's precisely the problem.' Liza eyed him warily as he stood there, hands in pockets, watching her. 'Where I'm concerned, I suspect you're capable of joking about anything. And you're certainly capable of messing me about.'

'Messing you about?' He continued to smile at her. Then he shrugged. 'Well, I can assure you I'm not messing you about this time. But it scarcely matters, does it?' He proceeded to stride past her. 'Since you've already decided to go straight back to London.

'Though it's a pity,' he added, flicking her a quick glance across his shoulder. 'As I've told you, the ballroom is really quite stunning. Very definitely worth a look.'

At the foot of the wide, curving staircase, he paused and turned to hold her eye for a moment. 'I'll make sure the money you're owed for the work you've done is waiting for you on your desk for you to pick up before you leave.'

He smiled a thin smile. 'Again, thank you for your help tonight. And now I think all that remains is for me to wish you a safe trip back to London.'

And then, without another glance at her, he proceeded up the stairs.

Well, this was a fine dilemma she'd been landed with!

Upstairs in bed Liza tossed and turned endlessly, knowing she'd be lucky if she managed to snatch an hour's sleep. Should she go or should she stay? What about her promise to Elliott? And what about her promise to her Great-aunt Julia?

She knew she ought to stay, for Aunt Julia's sake. But, quite unaccountably, she felt afraid. Richard's sudden turnaround somehow felt like a trap.

What kind of a trap? she asked herself impatiently. You're being stupid. There's nothing to be afraid of. But then she started thinking about Elliott...

She'd promised Elliott she'd go back with him and she hated to go back on that. Though he didn't know it, hadn't she already let him down enough?

Hadn't she let him down tonight when she'd allowed Richard to kiss her again? Didn't she let him down virtually every time she looked Richard in the face? For it was getting to be that bad. She could scarcely even look at Richard without responding to him in a way that shamed her to the core. For she did not care for him. It was just a physical reaction. How could she possibly care for a man who was only playing with her anyway and who was nothing but a skirt-chasing Don Juan?

She sighed and closed her eyes. There she went again, trying to rationalise away her feelings when, surely, there were no feelings worth rationalising away? All she felt for Richard was foolish attraction. Nothing deeper. The only man she felt deeply for was Elliott and it was Elliott she ought to be thinking of now. The last thing in the world she wanted was to hurt him or to put at risk the relationship they had.

And I shall do that if I stay, she thought in tormented misery. That's why I must leave, and leave immediately. Then she remembered again—but what about Aunt Julia and the ballroom?

In the end, she decided there was only one thing for it. She had already set her alarm for eight-thirty. As soon as it went off, she would phone Elliott at his hotel, put her dilemma to him and let him decide for her.

'You've come for your money? Mr Hawkes asked me to give you this.' Penny smiled a little sadly as she held out a cream-coloured envelope and told Liza, 'We'll all be sorry to see you go.'

'I'm not going—yet.'

Liza smiled a little awkwardly. She'd only stopped by the office because she'd seen Penny's car, not in order to pick up her money. She'd just wanted to say hello and ask the other girl how long she'd be staying. As she'd guessed, Penny had come in, in spite of the fact that it was a Sunday, as a simple gesture of moral support in the light of last night's fire.

Liza told her now, 'I need to have a word with Mr Hawkes. Where can I find him? I suppose he's down at the stables?'

Penny nodded. 'He's been down there since early this morning. There's a bunch of police and detectives with him.'

'Thanks.' Liza nodded. 'I'll see you later,' she told Penny. 'And, in the meantime, I'd be grateful if you'd just hang on to that envelope.'

It took fifteen minutes' brisk walk to get down to the stables and Liza could see as she approached it that it was a hive of activity. There were a couple of police cars and a large white builders' van parked alongside Richard's Range Rover, and there appeared to be men everywhere, some measuring and hammering, others on hands and knees searching around in the dirt.

At first, she couldn't see Richard as she stood on the sidelines and searched for him, a little reluctant just to barge in when they were all so obviously busy. But then suddenly she spotted him stepping out of one of the stables, deep in conversation with the plain clothes detective at his side.

And it was uncanny the way her heart leapt and seemed to lodge in her throat for a moment as she looked into his handsome, dark-eyed face. In that moment it was as though the sky had grown a little brighter. Something deep inside her seemed to shimmer.

Fool, she told herself, dropping her gaze away hurriedly and staring for a moment, hard, at the ground. You find him exciting, that's all. Exciting and dangerous. And you don't need dangerous. Elliott's what you need.

By the time she glanced up again, she had recovered from her madness. Which was just as well, for he was walking towards her.

'Shouldn't you be on your way back to London?' As he addressed her, his expression was uncurious and unsmiling. 'What's the matter? Do you have some complaint about the money I left for you?'

'No, it's not that...' Liza stepped back a little awkwardly as he swept right past her and headed for the Range Rover. Clearly, he hadn't come over to speak to her at all! She hurried after him. 'I want to talk to you... I've decided not to go back today, after all.'

'Oh?' He seemed less than riveted by this news. 'I thought you were desperate to go back with Elliott?'

'I am, but... Well, I've decided to stay on for another day. That is, if——'

She let her voice trail off. It felt rather like talking to a piece of wood, for Richard was paying her not a blind bit of attention. As he reached the car, he pulled the door open and leaned inside to retrieve a plastic bag.

'Breakfast,' he observed, pulling out a cheese roll wrapped in cellophane and a Thermos flask, which he proceeded to twist open. 'And not before time,' he added with a sigh of satisfaction, as he poured steaming black coffee into the Thermos top and drank.

'You mean you haven't eaten all morning?' Liza regarded him with sympathy. She, at least, had taken the time for a bowl of cornflakes and a cup of coffee before coming out. 'You must be starving. It's nearly ten o'clock!' She narrowed her eyes curiously. 'How long have you been out here?'

'Since about six o'clock. I had to see to the horses. I wanted to be sure they were OK after last night's little scare.'

Liza blinked at him. 'Good grief! I thought I was up early! You must have had only a couple of hours' sleep!'

'It felt more like a couple of minutes.' Richard smiled a wry smile and took a large hungry bite of his cheese roll. 'Thank heavens for Penny,' he added, chewing. 'She was good enough to think of bringing me some breakfast.'

'That was most thoughtful.'

Liza felt oddly irked. *I* should have done that, she found herself thinking. *I* should have been the one to bring him breakfast. Though it was a ridiculous thing to think. Where had such a silly thought come from?

She dismissed it instantly and changed the subject. 'So, what's been going on here?' she enquired with a nod at the stables. 'Have the police made any progress as far as figuring out how the fire was started?'

'Nothing conclusive.'

As Richard smiled at her, Liza sensed he had picked up that abrupt change of subject. She wondered if he had also guessed what had prompted it and was aware of a very slight reddening of her cheeks. If he had, he must think her even crazier than she did!

But now, he in turn proceeded to change the subject. He took another mouthful of his coffee. 'So, what were you saying about having changed your mind about going back to London today?' He paused and eyed her with amusement. 'I must say that's a most unexpected development.'

'It's not so strange.'

Liza felt oddly defensive. Did he think she had changed her mind because of him? Did he think she was about to become yet one more conquest? Just in case he did, she put him right straight away.

'I decided to stay on because of what you said last night—about having decided finally to let me see the ballroom. But just for one day. That should be more than long enough. And then I'll be on my way back to London as planned.'

It was all so simple and so logical, she thought as she told him. Not at all complicated and hopeless like it had felt last night. And she had realised just how straightforward the solution really was when she'd awakened this morning, suddenly clear-headed and calm again, just a couple of minutes before the alarm went off. It seemed astonishing that last night she hadn't been able to see it. But last night she'd been tired and overwrought.

Elliott had been in full agreement with her when she had phoned him.

'Of course you have to stay on and see the ballroom,' he'd insisted. 'And I'm delighted to hear that Hawkes has finally come round. Though I'm sorry,' he'd added, 'that you won't be coming back with me. Still it's just one day. I think I can probably survive.

'And just think,' he'd added with a smile in his voice. 'We'll be able to go to that concert on Friday. It'll be back to our old familiar routine. I'm really looking forward to it.'

'So am I.' Liza had breathed a sigh of relief. 'It'll be great to finally get away from here.'

Now she told Richard, 'I hope there's no problem? I hope you haven't changed your mind about letting me see the ballroom, after all?'

'You hope I'm not messing you about, you mean?' An amused flicker touched his eyes. But then, abruptly, his expression sobered. 'If you can think such a thing, you obviously have no idea of just how grateful I am for the way you helped me last night.'

As she looked back at him, Liza's heart twisted inside her with emotion. She wanted to tell him, 'It was nothing,' but that look of dark intensity in his eyes had made the words choke in her throat.

And as he continued to frown at her, she could sense very strongly that a million different thoughts were going round in his head. And, suddenly, she was afraid even to wonder what they might be. And even more afraid that one of them might reach out and touch her.

Without taking his eyes from her, Richard laid his coffee-cup on the car roof and with his free hand reached out softly to touch her cheek.

'I owe you,' he told her. 'So the very least I can do for you is make your dearest wish come true.' Lightly, playfully, he tweaked the end of her nose. 'I promise you, my dear Liza, you shall go to the ballroom.'

Idiot! Liza smiled back at him. 'Who do you think you are? My Fairy Godmother?'

'Fairy Godmother... Fairy Godfather... Whichever you prefer. Either way, I suspect it's probably a vast improvement on the way you've thought of me up till now. You've probably thought of me as the two Ugly Sisters rolled into one.'

'Close.' Liza pulled a face at him. She could not deny it. 'One thing's for sure—you've been no Prince Charming!'

It was an innocent enough joke, but Liza wished she hadn't made it. The words were no sooner out than she regretted them. They had sounded almost like a complaint!

And the knowing way Richard looked back at her only made her feel worse. 'Haven't I?' he smiled. 'That's most unlike me.'

It was really rather a blessing that at that precise moment they were interrupted as one of the plain clothes detectives came alongside them.

'Excuse me,' the man said, addressing Richard. 'I think we've just about finished now. We'll get off and let you get on with clearing up.'

'Thanks, Inspector.' Richard turned to face the man. 'Have you managed to come up with anything else?'

'A couple of things. We've got a pretty good shoe print and I think we may have found the remains of the rag that was used to start the fire. Along with that brass button you found, they may help to point us in the right direction. Let's hope so, anyway.' The Inspector began to head for his car.

'And thank you for all your co-operation, Mr Hawkes.'

'My pleasure, I assure you,' Richard told him as he accompanied him.

Liza watched as they shook hands before the Inspector drove off. Brass button? she was thinking, wondering why that rang a bell. But she had already dismissed it from her thoughts by the time Richard returned a moment later, finishing off the remains of his cheese sandwich.

'Now that the police have finished raking over the area for evidence, I can tell the builders to get on with what they're here for. Up until now they haven't been able to do much more than a bit of measuring.'

As he spoke, he took his coffee-cup from where he'd left it on the car roof, quickly drained it and screwed it back on to the Thermos flask.

'I'll keep the rest for later,' he winked, pulling open the car door and dropping the flask inside. 'And now, I must leave you. I have work to do,' he said.

'But I'm here to work, too.' As he was about to step past her, Liza stepped forward, blocking his path. 'Tell me what I can do to help.'

'I think what you should do is go back to bed and have yourself another couple of hours' rest. I know that's what I would do if I were in your shoes.' He smiled down at her. 'Go on. I reckon you deserve it.'

'I wouldn't dream of it.' Liza shook her head. 'I'm here to help, so you'd better tell me what to do.'

Richard raised one dark eyebrow and observed her for a moment. 'OK, since you insist, I'm sure we can find something for you to do.' Then he tilted his head. 'You know, I'm impressed. I'd no idea you'd developed such a strong sense of commitment to Abbotsdale Castle Estate.'

'I haven't.' As he turned away, Liza felt oddly caught out. 'It's only until tomorrow. Just for as long as I'm here,' she hurriedly assured his already retreating back. 'After tomorrow, I won't even remember this place.'

I won't, she assured herself. I'll never give it another thought.

But as he turned to flick her a quick glance over his shoulder, she had to catch her breath and drop her gaze away.

It was a busy, hectic, but deeply satisfying day. So much had been achieved, it was unbelievable.

All the mess had been cleared up and most of the damaged roof rebuilt. The horses' stalls had been returned to their usual state of order and they'd even managed to find time to exercise the animals as usual.

'I would definitely say we've earned our supper tonight,' Richard smiled as they climbed into the Range Rover just before seven and headed back along the road to the castle. 'In fact, I'd even say we deserve a celebratory bottle of champagne.'

'I'll drink to that.'

Liza's tone was light-hearted, but deep inside she was feeling wistful. She leaned back in her seat and gazed out of the window. It was hard to take in that the day had passed so quickly and that by this time tomorrow she'd be back in London. There'd been an oddly timeless feeling about today. As though it would never draw to an end.

She shook her wistfulness from her. There was nothing to feel wistful about. It was good that the day had passed so quickly and that she'd soon be on her way back to London and Elliott.

'By the way, I haven't forgotten, even though I haven't mentioned it again.' As Richard spoke, Liza turned in her seat to look at him. 'I mean,' he explained, 'about showing you the ballroom.'

'The ballroom? Ah, yes.' Liza nodded and turned away again. She hadn't forgotten either, though neither had she much thought about it. She'd been far too busy to think of such things.

'I've decided to let you choose when you want to go and look at it.' They'd reached the castle courtyard and Richard was parking the Range Rover. 'Before dinner or after dinner? Whichever you prefer.'

Liza pondered for a moment. 'I think before,' she told him.

'That's what I thought, too. We can get it out of the way then and enjoy a nice leisurely dinner together afterwards.'

That sounded a little cosy, and it was not, Liza quickly assured herself, even remotely the reason why she had made her decision. She simply wanted to get into the ballroom as quickly as possible, before he had a chance to change his mind again!

She turned a sharp glance on him. 'I'll want to spend a bit of time. I don't want to be rushed. And, of course, I'll want to take some photographs.'

Richard did not argue. 'Of course,' he agreed equably. 'You shall take your photographs and have all the time you need.' He glanced at his watch. 'Do you think an hour will be enough? Shall I tell Mrs Donnelly to have dinner on the table for eight-thirty?'

Liza nodded. 'OK.' That sounded reasonable.

Richard was climbing down from the car and leading the way across the courtyard. 'In that case,' he said, 'I suggest we go our separate ways now, and meet in the drawing-room in about half an hour's time.'

Then he caught her eye as he stood aside to let her pass ahead of him through the stone porch. 'I'll be waiting to welcome you with a glass of champagne.'

Upstairs in her room Liza showered quickly, then frowned into the wardrobe, wondering what to wear.

Her gaze kept flickering towards the jade-green dress, the most stylish of all her clothes and very definitely her favourite. And why not? she kept asking herself. This was a special occasion. She was finally going to see the ballroom!

Yet she hesitated. Richard might get the wrong idea. He was vain enough to think she was wearing it for him. And that was the last thing she wanted. Tonight, on her last night, she definitely wanted no misunderstandings, especially of the kind that could lead to problems. And, by problems, she was thinking of the kissing variety!

She detached her gaze from the jade-green dress and scanned the row of hangers. Something a little less flattering, a little less eye-catching, a little more sober was what was called for. Something that would look as though she'd just flung it on at random and didn't particularly care about the way she looked.

Her hand reached for the beige skirt that she normally wore with a plain white blouse. This would be perfect, she decided, pulling it out.

But she felt oddly deflated as she stood and examined it, and in spite of herself her eyes strayed back to the green dress. After all, she argued, it wasn't really so special. It was a favourite of hers, but that time she'd worn it with Elliott he hadn't even considered it worthy of comment.

She smiled a satisfied smile and shoved the beige skirt back on the rail. She would wear the jade dress. She would wear it for Aunt Julia. It was Aunt Julia, after all, who'd said it made her look like a million dollars and she'd be tickled to know she'd worn it on her visit to the ballroom.

It was just after half-past seven when Liza hurried downstairs, her camera slung in readiness over her shoulder, and made her way confidently across the hall to the drawing-room. She was feeling good. In fact, she was feeling terrific. Tonight, she was finally going to get what she'd come for. And tomorrow she'd be leaving, still in one piece. For tonight—she had no doubt of it—she'd have no trouble handling Richard!

He was waiting for her, as promised, in the drawing-room, sitting back casually in one of the armchairs, dressed in a dark suit and contrasting cream shirt. But his gaze was fixed elsewhere as Liza appeared in the doorway and, just for a moment, he didn't see her.

And in that moment as, unseen, she watched him from the doorway, Liza felt her breath catch painfully inside her. This is our last evening together, she thought in sudden anguish. After tomorrow I shall never see him again.

With an almost frantic urgency, she drove these feelings from her. Where had they come from? She had no business feeling them!

In that very same instant Richard turned to meet her gaze and smiled at her. 'Wow,' he murmured appreciatively. 'You look terrific!'

He should not have said that. Something tore at Liza's heart. She had to swallow hard and count up to ten before she felt sufficiently in charge to reply to him.

'This old thing? I always wear it for farewell dinners.'

Her tone was so off-hand it was almost brittle and she hated the sound of it in her ears. But she had to be off-hand. It was the only way she could cope.

She looked into Richard's eyes and added, 'This is my farewell dinners dress.'

'If I'd known, I'd have been looking forward even more to the evening.' He smiled a smile that was impossible to fathom. Did he care, Liza wondered, that she was leaving? It was quite impossible to tell.

Then he indicated the bottle of champagne in the ice bucket on the table. 'Shall we crack it open now or wait till you've seen the ballroom?'

'Let's wait.'

Liza was suddenly feeling all tense and off balance. A moment ago she'd been feeling terrific, but now she felt upset and confused. Why should she care whether he was sorry to see her go or not? And why this sudden weight, like cold cement, that seemed to have settled in the pit of her stomach?

'I'd prefer to go and see the ballroom first.'

'Very well, then.'

Without hesitation, he was rising to his feet. Then he was leading the way across the drawing-room, with Liza following in his footsteps, wondering how she could possibly be feeling so wretched when the prize she had so longed for was about to become hers.

At least there was no doubt about one thing. The ballroom was spectacular.

It was a huge room, hung with glittering chandeliers, with magnificent carpets, like colourful jewels, strewn over the polished parquet floor.

'It's unbelievable!' Liza gasped as she stepped inside, in her wonderment instantly shedding all the turmoil inside her. 'I've never seen anything like it in my life!'

'Then snap away.' Richard smiled indulgently, as he seated himself on one of the silk-covered armchairs. 'I hope you remembered to bring plenty of film.'

Liza shot two rolls of film and she could have shot more. She was so entranced she could have gone on shooting all night. But at last she flopped down on the armchair next to Richard. 'I think that's more than enough!' she laughed.

'Are you sure?' While she'd been snapping, he'd been watching her with fascination, explaining what things were, giving her a little of their history and pointing out some of the best angles for her pictures. 'You're more than welcome to carry on,' he told her now. 'I can call down and ask Mrs Donnelly to hold dinner for a while.'

'Is it really that time already?' Liza glanced at her watch. 'I can't believe it! It's twenty past eight!' Then she shook her head. 'No, thanks. I've got enough here. Though there is something...' She paused and narrowed her eyes and nodded towards a group of portraits that hung on the far wall. 'I'd like to have a closer look at those.'

'Go ahead.' Richard nodded. 'We've got time.'

Liza rose to her feet, swinging her camera over her shoulder, and made her way across the huge room. Then when she came close to the portraits she paused and stared hard at them. Something about one of them had caught her eye earlier while she'd been zooming around with her camera, and she wanted to check whether she'd been mistaken.

And now as she stared, it seemed she must have been. It must have been a trick of the light or something. She was about to turn away and then suddenly she saw it. She stopped dead, her eyes almost popping out of her head.

It wasn't a trick of the light! She hadn't been seeing things at all!

And then a voice spoke behind her, making her jump. 'Handsome chap, wasn't he?' It was Richard, come to join her.

Liza spun round to look at him, her eyes wide with wonder. 'It could be you!' she gasped. 'That guy in the painting's your image!'

'Apart from the velvet jerkin and the frill around his neck.' Richard met her gaze with a teasing smile. 'And I promise you, my hair's never been quite as long as his.'

'But, all the same, it could be you—apart from these small details.' Liza gasped. 'It's uncanny. It's like looking at a picture of you in fancy dress!'

She turned to him. 'He's obviously one of your ancestors!'

'One of the big bad Hawkeses who persecuted your family?' Richard smiled a teasing smile, then suddenly his smile softened. 'You're right, this man in the painting is my ancestor. My great-great-great-grandfather was his bastard son.'

'Bastard son? You mean you're not a legitimate heir, then?'

'I'm no heir at all.' Richard shook his head at her and reached up suddenly to touch her cheek with his fingers. 'In fact, it's sheer coincidence that I bear the name Hawkes at all.'

Liza was watching him with rapt attention, her eyes fixed on his face, but, really, she was only half listening to what he was saying. She was lost in his nearness, in the touch of his fingers, in those beautiful dark eyes of his with the grey and amber flecks.

Funny, she was thinking, it feels like a very long time since I thought of him as one of the big bad Hawkeses. If I ever really did. He's really always just been Richard.

She said, 'So, how did you come to end up as the owner of Abbotsdale Castle?'

'Another coincidence, or maybe it was fate.' Richard's expression was soft as his fingers stroked her face. 'I bought it when it came on the market about five years ago, principally because it was perfect for my needs—and also because the idea of owning it greatly appealed to me. This place once belonged to a powerful family who did a lot of people a lot of harm.

'Not just the Blakes...' He smiled and touched her hair. 'But also my family... Particularly my great-great-great-grandmother. She was a servant in the castle, seduced and then abandoned. The Hawkes family ruined her life.

'So, you see... You and I have a lot in common. More than just a love of horses.'

As he paused and held her eyes, Liza's heart was hammering. We have nothing in common, she tried to tell herself. But that thought was drowned out by the emotions that poured through her, and by the certainty that suddenly filled her. He's going to seduce me, she thought in panic. And I'm going to let him.

His hand slid down softly to curl around hers. 'Shall we go down now?' he was saying. 'Dinner will be ready.'

Then he was leading her across the ballroom, beneath the chandeliers, and Liza was following him, as though in a kind of dream. Aglow with heady excitement. Riven with fear.

This is it, she was telling herself. How will I ever resist him after a dinner laced with champagne and seductive conversation? I'll never do it. I'll be totally at his mercy. I shall end up betraying Elliott totally.

They had descended the curving staircase and now he was leading her across the hallway to the dining-room where a hundred candles flickered. As they stepped into the room, he paused and smiled down at her.

'There,' he said, 'what do you think of that? It's in your honour. A combined thank-you and farewell dinner.'

The room looked wonderful, the big mahogany table bright with sparkling crystal and silver. It's magical, Liza thought, feeling her anxiety suddenly vanish and only the shimmering excitement remain. And it's going to be a magical evening.

She turned to smile at Richard, suddenly feeling wonderfully reckless. But in the moment she met his eyes, like a bolt from the blue, freezing her to the spot, something popped into her head.

The brass button! Suddenly, she knew why it had rung a bell with her earlier!

She frowned at Richard. 'That button you found at the stables? Exactly what sort of button was it?'

'It was a plain brass button. The type you get on a blazer.' He was frowning at her. 'Why on earth do you want to know that?'

Liza sighed. 'Because I've suddenly remembered something. I saw a man wearing a blazer with brass buttons down near the stables yesterday. I'll bet it's the man who started the fire.'

'Can you remember what he looked like?'

'Yes, I can. Vividly. I was riding Ken's bike and I almost ran into him. I can remember his face very well.'

There was a long, pregnant pause as Richard looked down at her. 'You know what this means?' he put to her finally. 'We'll have to contact the police so you can tell them all about it...'

He reached out and touched her cheek, his eyes narrowing as he continued, 'Either we can do it tonight, which we must if you're leaving tomorrow...or you can put off your departure and we'll contact the police first thing in the morning...'

He continued to hold her eyes. 'The decision is yours.'

Liza held her breath, finding it hard to hold his gaze. From the corner of her eye, she could see the dinner table waiting for them, the champagne on ice, the flickering candles. And in her mind's eye she could see all that was destined to follow this romantic dinner that he had laid on for her.

And for a moment she was tempted to give the

answer she knew he wanted—the answer that, to her shame, she herself wanted to give.

But, even as she hovered on the brink of temptation, she somehow managed to pull back just in time.

She dropped her eyes to the carpet. 'I guess we'd better call them now.'

CHAPTER NINE

IT WAS after midnight when Liza finally flopped into bed, exhausted, but relieved at the way the evening had gone. For there had been no seduction, nor even anything similar. Virtually the entire evening had been spent down at the local police station.

In the end, they hadn't even opened the champagne, though they had managed to snatch a couple of bites of dinner in between all the shuttling about and interviews that had followed. For Richard had phoned the inspector right away. He hadn't even tried to change Liza's mind and persuade her to stay on for another day.

'OK,' he'd agreed with a shrug. 'If that's what you want.'

It was what she wanted. Once she'd come to her senses, Liza was quite sure of that. And it was a huge relief to her that, just in time, she'd been snatched from the jaws of an ignominious fate. For she'd already been halfway down the slippery slope. To her abysmal shame she could not deny that. If it hadn't been for that timely recollection, she might very well have ended up in Richard's bed.

Shame on you, Liza Blake! she chastised herself.

As it was, nothing even remotely in that line happened. The inspector arrived within twenty minutes of Richard's phone call, while they were picking in strained silence at a dish of chicken and red peppers.

Then there followed another forty minutes or so of questioning, until the inspector finally said, 'If you don't mind, Miss Blake, I think it would be a good idea if you came down to the station for an hour. Your description of that man you saw sounds familiar. I'd like you to have a look at some of the mug-shots in our files.'

'Of course.' Liza was only too eager to oblige. She rose to her feet. 'Ready when you are.'

'I'll come with you.' Richard had spoken. 'Miss Blake can ride with me in my car,' he told the inspector. 'It'll save you having to bring her back later. And, anyway, I'd like to be there.'

And so the three of them set off for the police station five miles away, and, though Liza and Richard made an effort to act normally, the atmosphere between them had altered dramatically. Every word they exchanged had a strained, false ring to it. Barely once did they actually meet one another's eyes.

He can't wait for me to leave now, Liza found herself thinking. Now that he knows there's going to be no seduction, he really can't wait to see the back of me. Well, that's fine by me. I can't wait to be gone, either. And, thank heavens, I came to my senses in time.

Her session down at the police station couldn't have gone better.

Over a cup of instant coffee the inspector plied her with a selection of photographs from the district's bulging known criminals file. Liza pored over each one carefully, before shaking her head. They were all of the same physical type she had described to the inspector, but none of them so far was the man she'd seen. Then at last the inspector handed her one that made her sit up straight.

'This is him. No doubt about it! Those heavy-lidded eyes and that gingery hair. This is definitely the man. I'd recognise him anywhere!'

The inspector had smiled with satisfaction. 'Yes, I thought this would be him. We have another two witnesses who also saw him. He's a crank with a history of setting fire to things—though sending threatening letters to his victims is a new development, which is why we didn't latch on to him sooner.'

He looked at Liza. 'I could have shown you his photograph first, but I had to be sure I wasn't putting ideas into your head.'

'Oh, there's no fear of that. This is definitely him.'

'Well done.' Richard, who had remained silent for most of the time, smiled at her now, a genuine smile of congratulation. And, just for a moment, as their eyes met and held and the warmth in his seemed to reach out towards her, Liza was aware of a plummeting sense of misery.

He's lost to me forever now, she found herself thinking. And though it was a bizarre thing to think—she had never wanted him, anyway!—the sensation of loss that thought sent rushing through her proved ridiculously hard to push away.

They'd driven back to the castle shortly before midnight, parked the Range Rover and walked across the courtyard in silence. But once inside the hall Richard had paused to ask her,

'Do you fancy a nightcap or something to eat? I asked Mrs Donnelly to leave something out, just in case.'

'I don't think so. No, thanks.'

In fact, Liza could have eaten. It had been a long day, with only a sandwich at lunchtime and a couple of hastily snatched scraps of chicken this evening. But she didn't want to hang around. Not with Richard. Better the pangs of hunger than that. For, suddenly, just being around him was making it impossible to think straight.

So she smiled vaguely and shrugged. 'I think I'll go straight to bed.'

'In that case, goodnight.' He held out his hand to her. 'I'll arrange for Jim to drive you to the station in the morning. I'll probably be busy with the builders down at the stables.'

'Of course.' Liza took his hand reluctantly. The thought of his flesh against her flesh gave her goosebumps. But she needn't have worried. He did not prolong the agony. His handshake was almost insultingly fleeting.

'Again goodnight. I hope you sleep well. And I wish you *bon voyage* for tomorrow.'

It was their second goodbye scene, Liza suddenly realised. The first, as it had turned out, had only been a rehearsal. But this one was definitely for real.

As the brutal truth of that sank in, she felt another lurch of sadness and had to tell herself sharply not to be foolish. The only emotion she should be feeling was relief.

She straightened her shoulders. 'Thank you. Goodnight.'

Then he was turning on his heel and heading for the drawing-room, leaving her standing alone in the hall.

Liza continued to stand there, very still, her hand still tingling from that brief contact with his, and watched until he'd disappeared through the doorway.

And she was aware of an uneasy sense of waiting—though of waiting for what she had no idea. Perhaps she was waiting for Richard to turn with one final glance at her, or perhaps she was waiting for herself to change her mind and go after him.

But neither of these two things happened. As the door closed behind him, feeling numb, like a sleep-walker, Liza made her way upstairs.

Five days had passed since Liza's return to London—though they'd been five days so heavy with misery they had felt more like five years. Every hour had been a penance. Every minute seemed to drag.

But tonight, she was telling herself, was going to be different. Tonight she was going to pull herself together and really make an effort to have a good time. For tonight Elliott was taking her to the Royal Festival Hall to hear the Schubert concert he'd bought tickets for.

She'd decided, very self-consciously, to wear the jade-green dress, the one she'd worn on that last evening at Abbotsdale Castle. Her instincts had told

her no. It brought back too many memories. These
days, each time she looked at it she felt a rush of
emotion. But that had simply made her all the more
determined to wear it.

She must overcome this madness that had over-
taken her and was drawing her down into a black,
bottomless pit. She must take control of her emotions. She must stop being so foolish. And the jade-
green dress was just a dress. Nothing special. Just
as none of her memories of Abbotsdale were special
either.

And so, just after seven, when Elliott rang the
doorbell, Liza hurried to answer it wearing the jade-
green dress, along with a smile that was determinedly cheerful.

She flung the door open. 'Hi!' she exclaimed.
'Come on in. I'm almost ready.'

It was a valiant effort, she reflected later, but
sadly it was no more successful than any of its recent
predecessors. As she looked into Elliott's face, she
felt only wretchedness, as something plummeted
despairingly inside her. She wanted so desperately
to feel pleased to see him. But all she felt was disappointment. The only person she wanted to see
was Richard.

Elliott, thankfully, seemed not to notice. He
smiled at her and kissed her on the cheek. 'I'd bring
along a jacket, if I were you,' he told her. 'It's gone
a little cool this evening.'

'OK.' Still smiling, Liza darted into her bedroom
and snatched down a navy linen jacket from its
hanger. Then she paused as she caught sight of
herself in the cupboard mirror.

Her smile looked false, her eyes looked sunken and it was no wonder at all that, unlike Richard, on that last occasion when she'd worn the jade dress, Elliott had not told her she was looking terrific.

Terrible, not terrific, was more like the truth of it. A perfect mirror image of how she felt.

At that, she snapped back her shoulders and pulled herself together. You've no excuse, she told herself angrily, for feeling terrible. You've got absolutely nothing to feel terrible about.

Lifting her chin, she took a deep breath. Try harder, she told herself, or you'll end up ruining Elliott's evening. And he doesn't deserve that. He doesn't deserve your moping. And he's already had more than enough of it this week.

Her smile was a little more convincing as she stepped back into the sitting-room.

'OK. I'm ready. Let's go,' she said brightly.

They took a taxi to the concert hall on the South Bank of the Thames and joined the throng of music lovers waiting to go in. Then at last they were being shown to their seats in the front stalls and as the orchestra tuned up the lights began to go down.

It was only then that Liza allowed herself to relax. Sitting back in her seat, covered by darkness, with secret relief she let the smile slip from her face. Then she swallowed hard and closed her eyes and made no effort to shut out the images that sprang before her.

For she knew there was no point. It was always like this whenever she found herself alone or in private. She could not stop the images coming.

And the images that sprang before her were images of Richard. Richard on horseback that first day she'd met him. Richard galloping round the practice track on Thunder. Richard sitting with a glass of brandy in the drawing-room waiting for her. Richard looking into her eyes the instant before he kissed her.

They were endless and unstoppable, these images. The minute she relaxed they would come crowding in on her. And even when she fought against them and tried to keep them at bay, she knew they were still there, lurking in the shadows.

A thousand times she had told herself it was all her imagination. That she could control this thing. That it was just some kind of madness. That if she just tried a little harder she could push it away.

But she had tried—heaven knew—and all it did was grow stronger. Sometimes the images seemed more real to her than the real world all around her.

She clenched her fists in her lap now and cast a guilty glance at Elliott, who appeared to be happily lost in the Schubert. At least Elliott was unaware of the agony she was going through. He knew nothing of the images that obsessed her. He had no idea of the despair she felt each time she looked at him. He didn't know that the only face she wanted to see was Richard's.

And she would never see Richard's face again. She knew that and she accepted it, though knowing it and accepting tore her in two.

She would never see him, she would never touch him, she would never speak to him again, ever. Her memories, and her images, were all she'd ever have.

At that thought, as cruel as a knife, her fists clenched so tightly that she could feel her nails biting into the flesh of her palms. How can I bear it, she wept silently, when the truth is I love him, when all I want in this world is to be with him again?

For over the past five days she had finally forced herself to face the truth she had fought against for so long. It would do her no good, it was utterly hopeless, but with all her heart and all her soul she loved that handsome, intoxicating Englishman. And, as long as she lived, she knew she would love no other.

As tears crowded her eyes she made no attempt to stop them, but just sat there, consumed by her silent, private misery, and let them splash down her cheeks into the lap of her jade-green dress.

'Please, can I go round just one more time?' Liza adjusted her hard hat and smiled down at her friend. 'Just one more time. After all, it's my last day.'

Her friend smiled back at her and nodded. 'Of course you can. I'll see you back here in half an hour.'

Liza threw her a grateful smile. 'Thanks. You're a sport.'

Then, tightening the reins and sitting tall in the saddle, she guided the big bay gelding round in its tracks and headed at a trot back along the path between the trees.

'Come on, boy!' she encouraged, adjusting her riding crop. 'Let's have one last round together!'

It was a bright August day down in London's Hyde Park and here on Rotten Row, one little corner of the huge park where horsemen for decades had been coming to ride, Liza was feeling perfectly at home. Over the past week she'd spent a lot of time down on Rotten Row.

She'd come upon it by chance during a walk through the park and at the sight of all the horses her heart had stopped inside her. It had felt for a moment almost as though she was back at Abbotsdale Castle and for an instant she'd been tempted to turn around and flee.

But something had made her stay and then come back again and again. She found being there soothing in a bittersweet kind of way.

Pretty quickly she'd made friends with the bay gelding's owner, who had offered her her horse to learn to ride on. 'He's good,' she'd told Liza. 'A perfect beginner's horse. You won't have any trouble with him.'

For Liza had found herself suddenly filled with the desire to learn to ride. A crazy desire that seemed to have sprung from nowhere. She rather regretted now having turned down Richard's offer to teach her, for she had learned to enjoy being around horses.

After a couple of lessons she'd soon got the hang of it, and now she was starting to get pretty good. As soon as I get back to Philadelphia, she found herself thinking now, one of the first things I must do is find myself a riding school.

Liza smiled to herself. If only Richard could see her! But instantly, determinedly, she pushed that thought away. Thinking of Richard was fatal. All it did was release painful memories.

As the path narrowed a little she slowed down to a sedate walk. She was in no hurry, and it was so beautiful in the park. It would be a shame, this last time, not to enjoy it properly.

She held the reins loosely, drinking in the warm air. If it weren't for these memories, it would be a perfect summer's day. Then she shook herself. Correction. It *was* a perfect summer's day. She had her memories, and her demon visions, well under control.

At that moment there was a rustling sound behind her. Curious, Liza turned round as, out of the trees, stepped the tall, dark figure of a man. At the edge of the path he stood and looked up at her.

'Well,' he said. 'So, it was true, after all.'

For a split second, Liza very nearly bolted in panic. She was seeing things! Her visions had come back to haunt her!

But she knew it was no vision. This was flesh and blood reality. For standing before her, as handsome as ever and making her heart break just to look at him, was Richard.

She took a deep breath, blinked hard and composed herself, fighting back the giddy surge of wild hope that he had come here to find her and take her back to Yorkshire. She knew she was mad even to entertain such a hope.

'Well, now,' she replied, 'this is a surprise.'

In response, Richard smiled at her. 'I'm the one who's surprised. I thought you said nothing would ever get you on a horse again? But you look good up there,' he added. 'You suit being on horseback.'

Then he raised one dark eyebrow. 'Aren't you pleased to see me? You look as though you've just seen a ghost.'

'I rather wish I had. I think I'd prefer it to the real thing.'

'Would you? That's a pity.' His smile faltered for a moment. Then he took another step towards her. 'Well, I can't say I feel the same. I'm extremely glad to see you.'

'And why would you be glad?'

Liza wanted to back away from him. Every time she looked down at him she felt almost overcome by the panic that rose up in huge waves inside her. In her heart, more than anything, she longed to embrace him. She longed to leap down from the horse, throw her arms around him and tell him how miserable she had been without him.

But he was about to trip her up. Didn't he always? His being here, she could count on it, was not for the purpose she hoped.

Richard smiled. 'I've been looking for you,' he said.

'Oh?' She did not dare to ask him why. If she did, his reply would only hurt her.

And it seemed she was right. 'I have something to give you.' As she frowned, he reached into his inside jacket pocket and held up for her to see a cream-coloured envelope. 'You went away without your wages.'

The crash of disappointment nearly buckled her in two. Was that why he was here? To give her her money? A flood of pain and tears rushed inside her. She very nearly swung the horse round there and then and rode away.

But he would know if she did that. He would know what she'd been hoping. And she had too much pride to reveal herself so shamefully.

So, she tossed him a cool look. 'You needn't have bothered. I'd forgotten all about it. You should have saved yourself the trouble.' Then she narrowed her eyes at him as a question occurred to her. 'How did you know that I was here?'

Richard continued to look at her. 'Elliott told me. He told me you've been spending a lot of time here. Every afternoon, apparently.'

'And when were you speaking to Elliott?' Liza felt a guilty tug inside her, as she always did these days at the thought of Elliott. 'I wasn't aware that you and Elliott were in touch with one another.'

'We weren't. You're right. But I was trying to track you down...' As though by way of explanation, he held up the cream-coloured envelope again. 'And in the end it proved easier to track down Elliott through his bank and get him to tell me where I could find you.'

'I see.'

Her tone was tight. Liza was growing more and more anguished the more he went on with his explanations. He must be in London on business and had decided to take the opportunity to amuse himself with this small diversion. He surely couldn't believe she really cared about these few pounds he owed her? And, anyway, he could have mailed them.

She moved stiffly in the saddle, thinking maybe she should ride off, after all, and deprive him of his entertainment and save herself further agony. But, before she could, he took another step towards her.

'Elliott tells me you're leaving tomorrow,' he said.

'That's right.' Liza tried to look pleased. 'Tomorrow morning. Early.'

'So, it would appear I only just tracked you down in time.' Richard frowned. 'Surely, that's a little ahead of schedule? I thought you were staying until September?'

'I was. I've changed my plans.'

She glared at him with hurt and hostility. Why was he bothering to fake this sudden interest in her affairs?

Then he surprised her totally. He narrowed his dark eyes at her. 'Elliott tells me you two have broken up.'

'Elliott told you that?'

'Yes, he did. Is it true?'

Liza shifted again. 'What's it to you?'

Richard did not answer. He held her eyes with his. 'He also told me that, since you got back to London, you've almost become like a different person. No more a lover of the city life, it seems. These days you spend your time riding around Hyde Park, walking among the trees, communing with nature. Elliott said one would almost believe you were wishing you were back in Yorkshire.'

He knew too much and there was something far too probing about the way those eyes of his were fixing her. She could feel them picking behind her fragile shield of hostility to the aching vulnerability beneath.

Liza flicked at the reins, suddenly desperate to escape him, but too quick he had stepped forward and snatched them from her.

'Is it true?' he demanded. 'Was Elliott telling the truth?'

'Leave me alone! I don't want to talk to you!'

Vainly, Liza struggled to take control of the reins again. She couldn't bear to be subjected for one moment longer to this monstrous, agonising inquisition. If he cared, it would be different. But he was only making fun of her.

But there was no escape. He was holding the reins too tightly. In sudden desperation she lunged forward in the saddle to strike out at him with her riding crop.

But Richard was much too fast for her and, anyway, she lost her balance. Suddenly, as he was grabbing her, she was slipping from the saddle, and the next moment, in spite of her struggles, he was lifting her to the ground.

He held her so that she seemed to be hovering above it. 'Why did you break up with Elliott?' he demanded.

The force of his dark eyes was burning into her. Liza could not meet them. She turned her head away, struggling to get a footing so that she could pull away from him.

'It wasn't easy,' she protested. 'I hated to hurt him! He cared for me! And I cared for him! Though

I know that's something you could never understand!'

'So, why did you break up with him?'

Richard was insistent. He continued to hold her, his eyes burning like fire.

'Because I had to!' At last, Liza turned to look at him, her face torn with all the emotions that were pouring through her, her body aching from the tears she was fighting to hold back. 'I didn't care for him enough. There! Is that what you wanted! I didn't really love him! And I hate myself for hurting him!'

As the words poured out of her, her heart was breaking. She wanted to beat Richard. He was the cause of all this suffering.

But as she looked into his face suddenly all the violence in her was silenced. She had never seen such naked emotion in a pair of eyes before.

'Elliott may be a little hurt, but he'll survive,' Richard was telling her. 'He'll get over it. He'll find someone else.' His tone was gruff, suddenly close to breaking. Then he shook her gently. 'But I never would. Never, I promise you. For as long as I lived.' His eyes poured down on her for a moment. Then, almost roughly, he pulled her against him. 'I know that now. Without you, I would be lost.'

For a long moment as he held her, there was a breathless silence. Nothing stirred. Nothing moved. The only sound, it seemed to Liza, in the entire universe, was the rhythmic beating of their two hearts.

Then at last Richard drew away a little and, still holding her, gazed down at her. 'I love you, Liza

Blake,' he told her softly. 'Make me the happiest man alive and tell me you love me.'

For a moment Liza could barely speak. She looked back at him in wonder. Joy and adoration shone from her eyes. Then she nodded and smiled shakily. 'Oh, yes. I love you.'

'Truly?'

'Truly.'

'And will you come back with me to Yorkshire? Will you come back forever and be my wife?'

Liza sank against him and stood on tiptoe to kiss him. 'I will, Richard Hawkes,' she breathed. 'Oh, yes. I will.'

Then she was laughing and weeping and sobbing all at once as he swept her into his arms and kissed her.

'Ah, my favourite jade-green dress!'

As Liza walked into the room, Richard stepped towards her, a smile lighting his face.

'You're looking sensational as usual,' he told her.

'If I may say so, you're looking pretty sensational yourself.'

As Liza met his gaze, a blush touched her cheeks. Recently, sensational seemed to have become their favourite word. And suddenly she was remembering what had passed between them last night. The most sensational night of love she had ever known in her life.

It had been their first night back at Abbotsdale Castle.

'We have to go back,' Richard had told her. 'I need you to co-host a very special dinner. That one with the Kinskys that you promised to attend.'

Liza had frowned at him, confused. 'But that was two weeks ago, surely?'

'It had to be postponed. They had to fly over to Europe—which was convenient for me because of the fire. I'm much happier that they're coming after the rebuilding's been done.'

Then he'd caught her in his arms and bent to kiss her. 'But the very next day after the dinner, you and I are going to fly to Philadelphia and you're going to introduce me to all your family. Particularly that aunt of yours,' he'd joked, 'who hates the Hawkeses so much.'

'She won't hate you. That I'm sure of.' Happily, Liza had wound her arms around his neck. 'She'll adore you. They all will. How could they resist you?' She'd kissed him. 'After all, you're the most sensational man on earth.'

'Not a Don Juan, after all?' Richard had smiled as he teased her. For she had told him about the fears she'd had before, fears that she realised now had all been in her head.

As soon as she'd told him, he'd hugged her. 'Oh, Liza,' he'd chastised her, 'you should never have taken what I told you so seriously. Even when I made that silly joke about enjoying the chase too much, I was already halfway to falling in love with you. Why else do you think I kept making it so difficult for you to leave? I couldn't bear the thought that you might go.

'My sweet,' he'd sighed, kissing her, 'if only you knew how I adore you.'

And, last night, with his body, he had shown her. For he was the tenderest, most exciting, most wonderful lover. And much more than that. He was her private miracle.

As they had lain together in his huge bed at the castle, warm and naked, tingling for each other, it was as though every loose end in Liza's life had come together. As though every step she'd ever taken, every move she'd ever made, every word she'd ever spoken had been leading to this. Suddenly, all she'd ever needed and all she'd secretly yearned for, miraculously, was hers.

And now he stood before her in the doorway of the dining-room.

'Before our guests arrive, I have something for you,' he said.

'I need nothing but you.' Liza looked into his eyes. 'As long as I have you, there's nothing else I want.'

Richard kissed her. 'You have me. And you will always have me.' Then he reached into the pocket of his dark blue jacket and drew out a small red leather box. 'But, all the same, I would like you to have this as well.'

Liza could guess what it was, but she could never have guessed at its magnificence. As she lifted the lid, she let out a gasp.

'Richard, it's sensational!' she said.

'An emerald to match your eyes—though it's not half as beautiful.' As she continued to gaze at it, he lifted the ring from its velvet bed and slipped it on to the third finger of her left hand. 'I want the world to know,' he told her, 'how much I love you.'

Liza gazed down for a moment at the square-cut emerald, set in a circle of flawless diamonds, and suddenly her eyes were wet with tears.

She glanced up at him helplessly, her heart bursting with love for him. 'And how can *I* let the world know how much I love you?'

'Just wear the ring,' he told her. 'And be with me always.'

Liza fell into his arms and covered his face with kisses. 'I will,' she promised. 'I will. Forever.'

MILLS & BOON

Always & Forever

This summer Mills & Boon presents the wedding book of the year—three new full-length wedding romances in one heartwarming volume.

Featuring top selling authors:

Debbie Macomber ♥ Jasmine Cresswell
Bethany Campbell

The perfect summer read!

Available: June 1995   Price: £4.99

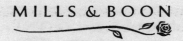

MILLS & BOON

are proud to present...

A set of warm, involving romances in which you can meet some fascinating members of our heroes' and heroines' families. Published each month in the Romance series.

Look out for "Simply the Best" by Catherine Spencer in July 1995.

Family Ties: Romances that take the family to heart.

SPRING FLOWER COMPETITION

How would you like a years supply of Temptation books ABSOLUTELY FREE? Well, you can win them all! All you have to do is complete the word puzzle below and send it in to us by 31st December 1995. The first 5 correct entries picked out of the bag after that date will win a years supply of Temptation books (*four books every month - worth over £90*). What could be easier?

L	L	E	B	E	U	L	B	Q
P	R	I	M	R	O	S	E	A
I	D	O	D	Y	U	I	P	R
L	O	X	G	O	R	S	E	Y
S	T	H	R	I	F	T	M	S
W	P	I	L	U	T	F	K	I
O	E	N	O	M	E	N	A	A
C	H	O	N	E	S	T	Y	D

COWSLIP

BLUEBELL

PRIMROSE

DAFFODIL

ANEMONE

DAISY

GORSE

TULIP

HONESTY

THRIFT

PLEASE TURN OVER FOR DETAILS OF HOW TO ENTER

HOW TO ENTER

Hidden in the grid are various British flowers that bloom in the Spring. You'll find the list next to the word puzzle overleaf and they can be read backwards, forwards, up, down, or diagonally. When you find a word, circle it or put a line through it.

After you have completed your word search, don't forget to fill in your name and address in the space provided and pop this page in an envelope (you don't need a stamp) and post it today. Hurry - competition ends 31st December 1995.

Mills & Boon Spring Flower Competition,
FREEPOST,
P.O. Box 344,
Croydon,
Surrey. CR9 9EL

Are you a Reader Service Subscriber?   Yes ❑   No ❑

Ms/Mrs/Miss/Mr _____

Address _____

_____

_____ Postcode _____

One application per household.   F

You may be mailed with other offers from other reputable companies as a result of this application. If you would prefer not to receive such offers, please tick box. ❑

mps
MAILING
PREFERENCE
SERVICE

COMP395